The Amazing Adventures of Dexter and Dood

H_2O
No armbands needed

S.L.Hill

This edition published in Great Britain in 2014 by:

Paws Publishing
Guisborough
Cleveland
UK

Email: matt@paws.pub
ISBN 978-0-9931519-0
December 2014

For all the children I have

had the pleasure to teach...

This book is for you!

CHAPTER 1

Kasper K.Itty was bruised and broken! He had fallen through the endless nothingness; dropping at an accelerated speed through the atmosphere, then the wispy clouds like a bullet from a gun and finally rested with an almighty PLOP! into a vast expanse of salt water where land was non-existent.

Kasper, similarly to most felines, wasn't too fond of water! Droplets that fell annoyingly from the grey clouds above were sufficient to turn Kasper's usual grumpy temperament into a roaring rage! However the current water problem was far greater. There was so much water that Kasper believed all of the green grass, brick buildings and catteries had been flattened and replaced by clear, salty liquid. 'Perhaps one of the thoughtless humans has left their tap on,' Kasper considered, as he hit the surface of the water with a resounding CRACK, similar to a weighty person belly-flopping from the ten metre diving board!

After being so rudely evicted from the grandeur of his cloud and control station of the entire universe high in the sky, Kasper's luck had taken a rapid turn for the worse.   Some months before he had stumbled rather cleverly upon a mystical jigsaw piece that granted wishes! (Yes I know... You are thinking where can I find such a thing!) Incidentally Kasper's greatest internal desire was to rule the world and for a short time, it looked like he would succeed.

But as with all great adventure stories, he was foiled at the last minute by two rather unlikely superheroes - Dood and Dexter! (We'll reintroduce you to them later!)

Meet selfish, nasty Kasper about to start a strop!

Down and down, what a mighty drop.

CHAPTER 2

As the biting coldness of the icy water shocked Kasper's ample frame, he started to panic as the surface of the water drifted away above him. His rapid descent through the depths of the ocean was swift, due to his weighty rear. The falling process had quickened and the darkness below engulfed him. Just as he was about to gulp his first mouth full of salty water, the seriousness of the situation seemed to jolt him and Kasper suddenly snapped into a frantic panic, moving his paws in a circular motion, flapping the dense water behind him. He pointed his head towards the surface above and cumbersomely attempted to propel his body forwards and upwards with frantic movements.

Defeated, as tiredness and exasperation took over, Kasper realised that his nine lives were finally up and he slowly gave up the fight to save his life. He lay back in the water, accepting of his fate and passing into kitty heaven, when his head suddenly collided sharply with something solid and pointy. Immediately, he turned his head to see a white cone shaped structure that looked like the root of a tree, suspended above him in the water.

As swiftly as a monkey, Kasper gripped his body around the white object and shimmied sprightly up the lifeline until it met with the surface of the water; where he gasped for breath. Kasper looked closely at the white form in front of him and realised that it was a large block of ice! He propelled his ten sharp claws, that had retired from action some years previously and hacked each of them into the ice like a pick axe, clawing his way out of the water and onto the icy surface above. He shook his whole body like a car wash roller and sat down on the irregular and slippery surface.

His breathing was rapid and laboured and he was completely exhausted! An hour or so previously he had been Ruler of the World sitting upon his cloud of splendour and riches; whereas now he found himself fighting to save his own life in an endless salty bath! He thought that today would go down as one of his less fruitful days!

Kasper composed himself, checked his body parts.... Two front legs, two back... One furry tail, ears and nose present - this completed his examination for now! He licked his left paw and began the washing process to remove all the salt from his orange fur, when the immenseness of his surroundings distracted him. All around him was ice, next to him, behind him and below him. Some sections were high and mountainous, others were flat and slippery. It was like one giant blob of ice cream, floating on the surface of an expanse of creamy milkshake.

Inquisitively, Kasper stood up and placed his extensive weight onto his paws, lifting his head to explore. Predictably, but as a shock to Kasper, the extent of the slippiness was uncovered, as all four paws rapidly moved outwards in the direction of the four compass points and he landed stomach first, straight onto the hard surface of the ice. Suitably winded and stars before his eyes, Kasper lay in this position and started to consider his options.

Slip and slide and twist in the air.

CHAPTER 3

"Come on Dexter, we have to get there early or you'll be spotted," Dood, the seven year old, ginger haired boy, commanded to a very reluctant and stubborn Dexter dog. Quickly, Dood put on his blue fleece coat and baseball hat to protect him from the biting cold outside his home, in a suburban ordinary street, in a town by the sea.

"How many times do I have to tell you Dood?" Dexter explained in a muffled tone from under the bed, "Dogs don't go to school! They snooze, woof and eat....simple!"

"Dex, I need you there buddy.... Just to get me through the science test! You can hover over Floral Fergie and check out the answers... It's the only way I'm ever going to pass!" he pleaded. Unsurprisingly, Dexter was a rather grumpy beagle that Monday morning. He was still tired from his greatly interrupted sleep the week before when he had stumbled upon magical powers and adventure far too immense for a novice superhero. Stubborn as a mule, he had refused to do anything at all other than sleep, eat and the odd short walk since and was quite sure he was going to maintain this stance for at least another week; maybe even a month or two! Even though he quite liked being a superhero, the experience had scared him a little. Dex and his young friend Dood, had quite literally been thrown straight into a real life disaster situation, that could have wiped out the whole universe. He considered that they both needed 'training' to be superheroes and that training would involve Grannies locked out of their houses or children stuck in toilets; nothing even slightly life ending and this was non-negotiable - he had decided! (Puppies can be very stubborn when tired!)

Exasperated and conscious of the time, Dood decided drastic action was necessary....he walked carefully out of his bedroom, avoided the water bomb suspended above his room door, grabbed one of Dexter's favourite sausage treats (normally only used at Christmas) and ran quickly down the stairs. Carefully stored high on a shelf, Dexter recognised the noise of the clasp releasing the top of the wooden box and immediately lifted his head and ran after his favourite treat. Stupidly, the door to Dood's room was left wide open, which was unusual due to the nosey crumblies and pro pink sisters that he lived with. They could potentially snoop around their adventure supplies, if the door was left momentarily ajar!

Out the door, Dood staggered, jumped and ran.

At that moment, Dexter was not his biggest fan.

CHAPTER 4

The deepest, bluest oceans that surrounded the green land masses of planet Earth nurtured an eco-system of creatures, great and small and luscious plants surrounded coral that were all colours of the rainbow. Zebra sharks, bottle-nosed dolphins, lion's mane jelly fish - to name a few, all lived in the extensive watery world hidden in the depths of the sea. Living corals provided shelter, green spindly sea weed and vibrant small fish and anemones allowed splendour and rich food.

One of the largest mammals, a blue whale, who happened to be called Barney, was leading his school of whales through the Arctic Ocean at the most northern part of planet Earth, near a land called Alaska. Sprightly, they swam at speed through shoals of multi-coloured fish, greeting each pack with a loud friendly "Good morning!" as they were, after all, the noisiest creatures in the ocean. Their chosen destination this morning was the old, twisted ship wreck that had sunk decades before near the abundance of icebergs that stood tall like skyscrapers, in the middle of the nothingness. The family of whales liked to play hide and seek amongst the wrecks, the ice towers and the masses of metal and rotting wood.

Over the years many ships had fallen foul in this area of the ocean. A city of icy towers stood like jail bars protecting the sea beyond. When ships had risked such a journey, their fate had often been disastrous (just like Titanic) and so the treasure upon the ocean floor provided engaging toys for the ocean creatures to play with.

Beauty, colour and wonder - enough said!

Along and over the deep, dark ocean bed.

CHAPTER 5

Kasper had surveyed his surrounding and it was bleak! He stood, slipped and fell at least a thousand times before he finally gave in and lay flat on his tummy, defeated. Despondently, he decided that to be able to move at all, he needed to find some skis or a gripping tool to aid his movement - unfortunately such shops were in short supply! He was about to consider a full scale paddy in frustration, when he looked up to the top of the icy mountain and something caught his eye due to the contrast of the colour - whatever it was - is wasn't white! Hopeful, he rubbed his eyes as the whiteness all around him was beginning to blind him, intriguingly on further examination there was indeed something there.

Rather un-cat-like Kasper had to resort to sliding along the ice like a seal, using his paws as paddles. Uneasily, he steered his body along the smoothest section of ice towards the bottom of the peak that contained the non-white interesting object. As he reached the summit he turned his head as best he could, towards the sky and squinted to see if he could see what was there. Kasper was still a rather lazy feline and if he didn't need to exert himself then he wouldn't!

Squinting hard at the whiteness against the constantly grey sky, he could just about make out a circular mass of what looked like twigs, decaying leaves, a possible sock and some pearlised shapes that could be shells. When he inspected closer still, he realised that he was looking at a nest of some kind and moments later he found out who the owner was. Swiftly, a graceful snowy owl swooped down into the scruffy nest, her mouth full of other treasures to add to her bed. As she dropped her find, she looked crossly over the side of the nest at the new creature below. Noisily, she tweeted something rudely that Kasper didn't understand, flapped her wings and flew off again once more, ruffling her feathers in a huff!

Kasper followed the snowy owl with his eyes, watching the bird getting smaller and smaller as she flew into the distance. Wearily, he took a deep breath and projected his claws out once more and started the ascent up the slippery mountain. Left paw first, he used his sharp claws to dig deeply into the ice, and using all his strength he pulled up his ample body, slowly sliding upwards towards the treasure at the top. Unfortunately, just as he was about half way up the icy mountain, Kasper foolishly decided to look down to see how far he had climbed (as he was feeling a little despondent). The shear height and the expanse of nothingness, apart from water were overpowering and his body began to shiver in fright. Sadly, this in turn caused the claws that were anchoring him firmly, to retract into his paws and all of a sudden Kasper found himself sliding at speed down the side of the mountain. Normally, this would have been an experience most people would have thoroughly enjoyed, like tobogganing, however Kasper just felt an overwhelming sense of sadness as he came to a halt at the bottom of the mountain, exactly where he started!

Amusingly, Kasper started his stroppy paddying movements that he used so frequently when he had an audience of mice servants to boss about upon his cloud. Even the fish and other creatures just below the surface of the water, weren't slightly bothered by the activity above and Kasper realised very quickly that he was truly alone in the world and there was no one out there to help him!

"What is that?" Kasper said, high in the sky.

With all his might, he didn't half try.

CHAPTER 6

The magical puzzle piece, the Divine piece of Creation, had started its decent from the clouds above when Kasper was foiled in his plan for world domination, some time previously. It moved swiftly through the atmosphere at such a speed that birds blinked in surprise as they believed something had sped past them but they could not see it! This piece had been guarded for many years by an old man named Old Rufus Rule; however it had been stolen by his evil and cruel cat, Kasper. Worryingly, the extent of magic this puzzle piece truly contained; nobody really understood! The only thing for certain was that this piece was integral to the formation of the universe and so consequently was the key to its sustainability and future.

As the piece neared planet Earth heading towards its next landing place, it appeared to swerve and navigate itself into the upper northern hemisphere, towards the icy climates of planet Earth. At intense speed the jigsaw piece hit the ice forming on the surface of the water with an icy CRASH! just as Barney the whale came up to the surface to take a look at the world above his watery home, in search of his next meal. As he yawned, he unknowingly swallowed the mystical jigsaw puzzle piece whole, in one gigantic gulp! It travelled down his digestive tract giving off a blue glow, as the water of the ocean had ignited its amazing magical power once more!

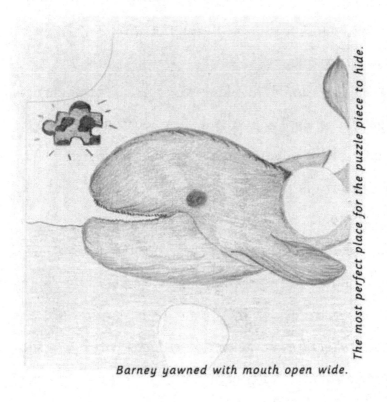

The most perfect place for the puzzle piece to hide.

Barney yawned with mouth open wide.

CHAPTER 7

Outside both Dood and Dexter were rather cold. The winter winds had taken hold and the morning frost had covered the buildings like a blanket.

"You didn't even give me chance to pick up my red coat this morning Dood! Call yourself a responsible owner!" Dexter muttered walking as slowly as he could, exaggerating his shivers, down the path outside their house.

"Dex, all you do, all day long is snooze.... Thirty minutes of your time is all I need and then you can curl up back on your bed for another ten hours! Lucky you I say! You need to see the amount of homework I have.... I'll be up all night tonight!" Dood explained, encouragingly.

Dood and Dexter were the best of friends. They ate, drank and slept together and most importantly shared two great bonds: 1) they were both ginger (only the greatest creatures in the world had been gifted with such a present) and 2) they both had a secret to keep - they were the hidden faces behind the world's newest and 'greatest' superhero team. It was just unfortunate that school and visiting Granny got in the way... And of course the fact that Dexter had refused to 'sneeze' and ignite his powers until they had had a little more training and rather frustratingly - he had completely 'slept back' all the hours of snoozing he had lost during their last scary adventure!

Dood was itching for more adventure but agreed with Dex slightly! Their flying had been well.... disastrous at best and they needed to find time around school stuff and sleeping hours to practise! Distracted, Dood noted to himself that maybe he would welcome yet another telling off about his lack of homework and spend his evening practising hovering and landing instead! He had searched 'Google' for such a manual but all that were available related to planes and bees; nothing even slightly dog related!

They arrived at the school gates an hour before anyone else. Mr Tranter, the whistling caretaker, was playing his usual tune, loud and strong to no one in particular but the winter birds seemed to enjoy the tones, as they sat on the branches preening their feathers before their first flight of the day. It was going to be easy to get into the school but the problem of avoiding the Headteacher could be more problematic! Her shiny red Mercedes was already parked in its regular parking space and Dood had heard the familiar 'clip clopping' of her heels, as she walked from her car across the empty car park into school.

Dood's school was old! Very old (almost as old as Granny) and in fact should be knocked down according to Dood. But its age was 'interesting' and 'added character' (according to Headteacher, Miss Snitch). Miss Snitch was a formidable character with a high pitched voice who liked to wear massive shoulder pads and scarves! Miss Snitch also had 'big' hair (excuse the lack of a more interesting adjective - but this is the best one to describe it. It was just big)! The other slightly odd thing was the way she smelled! She must spray at least one whole bottle of perfume from head to toe before leaving the house! Spending more than five minutes in her office, required breathing apparatus due to the fumes! Hence why she was secretly referred to as 'Stinky Snitch'. Dood should know; he did have a regular visitation slot most weeks! Everyone knew when she was coming due to her echoing footsteps, high pitched voice and laugh so loud, it could force buildings to crumble. However if she was laughing, severe punishments were about to be delivered, as she only laughed when something dastardly was about to happen!

The school itself was one long corridor. In the middle was the entrance and a turning left was for the young kids and right for the older ones! At the entrance, during the school day, sat Miss Richmond. She was the only kind and understanding school person he knew! She had often helped Dood when he got himself in a few scrapes and had selectively forgotten about them when asked by other adults! She had 'cool' status in Dood's mind and this was something rather hard to obtain!

Patiently, Dood and Dex waited behind the transparent cycle sheds for the right moment to enter the school building via the main entrance. All other entrances from the playground were still closed at this time. Worryingly, Miss Snitch's office was right by the entrance and they would have to sneak past her office to get in! As Dood waited, Dexter wandered off as usual, to sniff the new sniffs around school - they were different to the wood's sniffs and so he was totally distracted!

The longest, oldest building you ever did see. It is also the last, yes last, place Dood wants to be!

CHAPTER 8

Several hours later, a weary and dishevelled Kasper moved around his iceberg in a slightly more efficient way, learning from his disappointing sliding accident earlier in the day. He eventually reached the top of the mountain and precariously peered at the treasures in the nest at the top! Inside were a variety of interesting 'finds' that the snowy owl had stolen over last spring. A woollen sock with a Christmas pudding stitched into it, a variety of decomposing dry leaves, a wooden spoon, some netting (possibly from a fishing disaster), many thick twigs of varying sizes and a range of shells.

Perched unsteadily on the peak of the icy mountain, Kasper picked up all of the belongings, one at a time from the nest. He positioned them in an exact position so that they would carefully slide down the mountain, coming to rest on the flattest section of the iceberg at the bottom. Unfortunately some of the shells moved too swiftly and ended up in the water, however by the time he launched the final wooden spoon, he had mastered how to land the items in the same place at the bottom of the mountain with skill and precision. He only had the final problem of getting himself down the mountain, which he did in the most unfeline-like way. Kasper placed his claws back in the ice once more and slid down the surface on his tummy feet first, leaving scratch trails in the icy exterior! (He had seen this trick on Tom and Jerry and admired Tom's quick thinking and style!)

Kasper composed himself and sat up next to his new possessions. For the first time in a while, he felt a glimmer of hope and a little pleased with himself! Maybe he wouldn't die after all... However his tummy was telling him that he was very hungry! He had used up all his fat reserves over the last few days and he desperately needed to eat very soon. Echoing, his stomach gurgled and groaned as he reminisced about the fine milk, sardines and fish that he had grazed on only days before.

He sat on the cold floor and analysed his find! First of all he picked up the netting and saw that it was reminiscent of the nets that he once saw Old Rufus use over his vegetable patch to stop pests, such as greedy birds gobbling up his budding shoots. He wasn't sure what he was going to do with that, so he discarded it for now, throwing it over his left shoulder. Secondly he picked up the shells; four beautiful shells that he poked with his paw to check that they wouldn't crack. Clumsily, due to the annoying slippiness, he measured the shell size against the length of his weary front paws. By pure luck, his paw fit perfectly inside the smooth curve of the shell. At last he had something to feel a little more positive about! He picked up the other shells and they all fit the size of his paws! He gnawed at some of the netting edges, and after thirty minutes of looking like an able Blue Peter presenter, he stood up and admired his handy work: four perfect ice skates attached firmly to his paws. Old Rufus loved to watch programmes about ice skating and was obsessed with the Winter Olympics and so Kasper had watched the square box on the wall that demonstrated how these slidy things on his feet would work. After two hours of practising to be Torvill and Dean around his ice berg - he was convinced he could even try a flip! But decided that he should probably reserve his energy for a much greater cause!

Expertly, he slid back to his pile of treasures and came to a halt! Kasper reached down to pick up the sturdy wooden spoon. It was long enough for him to use as a ski pole, to poke into the ice as he slid, though he would have preferred to have another to keep him balanced; but knew beggars couldn't be choosers right now! He sat down once more on the edge of his iceberg looking out over the overpowering expanse of nothingness. All he could see was the horizontal line far away in the distance where the sea met the sky and the family of towering icebergs similar to his own new home. Hopelessly the view was the same hour after hour, day after day!

As he looked over the water, something below caught his attention. Through the surface of the water were small, strange movements. Inquisitively he investigated further and realised that metres below him was...... DINNER! Fish of varying sizes swam back and forth under his nose in families moving in wavy lines. Quickly he ran back to his treasure pile and began to construct a fishing net similar to the one used to catch grumpy old cats to take to the vet! The cogs in Kasper's brain began to turn once more! He felt like his luck was changing, at last!

slide around an iceberg without a sound?

Could something so furry and round,

CHAPTER 9

Through their hiding hole the adventurers looked on. "Maybe I should have just revised a bit more for this test..." Dood was beginning to think on reflection. Hidden, Dexter was still taking in all the new school related smells through the undergrowth of bushes and trees.

"Right, here is the plan... We need to move fast as the other kids will be arriving soon and that means possible 'rumbling' alert. So... we are going to crouch down on our knees, crawl under Snitch's window on the outside, through the door, past the office and stand just around the corner from the Headteacher's office so that we can check her whereabouts before we scarper down the corridor! Got it Dex!?" He explained to no-one in particular. Excitedly, Dood continued to look on, assuming Dex was just behind him. 'What do you think buddy?" he continued. Dood looked like he needed the toilet, jumping up and down from behind the shed, trying to find the right moment to move. Frustrated, he turned to see Dexter's rear high in the air. His four-legged friend was digging...soil was flying behind him landing in small piles as he focused on his find! "Dex! Come on, I need your help buddy." Distracted Dexter kept digging just a moment longer, but could sense Dood with his hands on his hips from the corner of his eye. Reluctantly he stopped digging and walked begrudgingly over to his friend.

"Dood, you wake me up, drag me to school in the freezing cold and then stop me finding my breakfast! It's a good job I love you mate!" he explained matter-of-factly, head hung in disappointment.

"Thirty minutes Dexter and you can dig up the whole field! Come on," Dood retorted as he skulked towards the school entrance. The duo looked funny. Precariously crouched, Dood walked almost on his knees commando style, like he was embarking on a furtive-based mission. Dex followed obediently, nose to the floor and tail down, so that they weren't spotted. Nearer and nearer they crept, under Snitch's outside window, through the front entrance, past the secretary's desk and arising to stand flat against the wall that adjoined Snitch's office and then all being well.... BINGO! they could run up the corridor to Dood's classroom.

With craned necks, the superheroes listened down the corridor for hoof noises but nothing! Not a sound. Prematurely, Dood was just about to exhale a huge sigh of relief before he embarked on turning the corner and prepare himself for the ten metre sprint. He edged his body round the corner, back against the wall like he was stuck with Velcro. As his body turned the ninety degree angle, something blocked his exit! It wasn't a book case, caution cone or giant plant. It was Snitch herself! Dood slid straight into her lamppost like figure, complete with hands on hips and lips so tight, she appeared as though she was sucking on a wasp!

Slowly, Dood looked up, which was tricky as he was far too close to someone who had 'teacher status.' Swift as a jack-in-the-box, Dexter heard the commotion around the corner, placed his four paw drive in reverse and scarpered away from the school gates as quickly as his legs would carry him!

"Ah now, Mr Redford... I had no idea that you loved school so much that you wanted to be here for an extra hour each day!" Snitch smiled, the widest most sarcastic smile. (Dood's real name was Joseph, but nick names from Granny stick for life... fortunately Doodle-doo had been shortened to Dood, which he could just about tolerate).

"Erm, you know me Miss, model pupil, I came to school early just to be sure I could cram in a few extra facts for today's exam!" Dood lied, rather flustered. (Dood unfortunately was the world's worst liar and turned the colour of a pillar box as soon as the lie left his lips).

Seemingly playing along with the most obvious deception, Miss Snitch answered, "That's excellent news Joseph, you can pop into the hall with me and help set up for your exam today, chop, chop!"

And off she trotted into the hall, pointing the way! Dood felt like he had been stung! Not only had he been rumbled, he had been caught red handed by his least favourite person. Head down, feet dragging, Dood walked into the hall knowing he was going to spend the next sixty minutes of his life, sharpening pencils and moving chairs! He was however relieved that Dexter had used his one brain cell to run away before he was caught too. Snitch didn't like dogs, especially ginger ones!

Whilst he was as free as a bird, Dexter took the opportunity to take the long way home, sniffing his favourite sniffs by the river bank.

Complexion pale, scary and getting whiter.

Can Snitch's lips get any tighter?

CHAPTER 10

Over the next few hours, Kasper found the energy to learn a number of new skills. Cleverly he used the wooden spoon and netting to make a simple fishing net. The dark colour of the netting was advantageous as it disappeared from view in the water and he hoped the fish couldn't see it either and would swim straight into it. He was so hungry by now that he felt quite dizzy. When he had tied the netting as securely as his paws allowed, he lay down stomach first on the ice, reaching over the side with his spoon and net in anticipation. He stretched it out over the water and began to sweep it through the icy water in a circular motion.

As he was such an impatient kitty, he expected to have five fine fish caught in his net within moments; but on closer inspection his dinner appeared to have disappeared. He stopped moving his net and looked through the glassy surface; nose almost touching the water. Annoyingly, a whole school of fish were glaring up at him in a mocking sort of way, just out of reach! "Meow! What am I going to do now?!" he thought despondently, not wanting to get wet again.

Feeling frustrated, he was aware that the sun was meeting with the horizon once more and he would be plunged into darkness and loneliness again. Woefully, he sat then lay onto his back, totally fed up with the situation that he was in. He left the net dangling into the water and closed his eyes. Kasper wasn't often a tearful cat but his eyes filled with salty fluid and he knew that the fight to save his own life was looking hopeless.

Dinner would be caught, who would have bet?

Over the icy edge he left the net.

CHAPTER 11

The rising sun woke Kasper as if it was his only friend. In all honesty, he had wondered if he would ever see the fire ball again as he was just so hungry, cold and tired. But his glowing friend greeted him once more. Slowly he sat up, achy from the biting cold in his bones. Disinterested he slid over to the water's edge where he had left his fishing net.... he felt so foolish to think that something so simple would actually work. Swiftly he pulled it out of the water and dragged it behind him onto the ice, taking no notice of what might be inside the netting. Kasper sluggishly dragged the net towards him and realised quickly that it was much heavier than the night previously and so he gave it an extra tug due to his annoyance about the whole situation. As he did so, he instantly heard a swish and flapping noise on the ice behind him. Delayed in his response, he slowly turned and observed an extensive pile of various sized fish and other sea creatures that had unknowingly found their way into Kasper's amateur lair.

Immediately, he dropped the pole and net combination and it fell to the floor with a loud 'CRACK!' Kasper's unsuspecting catch started to wriggle on the ice as they were taken from the comfort of the ocean and a flummoxed Kasper looked on, unsure what to do next. Stupidly, he stood up and flapped his arms above his head in a half joyous and half shocked expression. By now, he was starving from lack of food and was beginning to feel a little delirious. He jumped without thought onto the newly caught fish, that were flapping and squirming on the ice and grabbed as many as he could, pushing them forcefully into his gaping mouth, that hadn't tasted food for many days. He would have liked his fish to be poached with a little salt and pepper, but realised fine dining wasn't an option just now. He sat on the side of his icy home and felt the food slide slowly into his hollow tummy and felt happier than he had, in a very long time.

Kasper Kitty hungry and thin.

Luck is on his side, he knew he would win.

CHAPTER 12

Barney, the blue whale, had hidden himself just behind the steering column of the largest ship wreck on the deepest section of the ocean, amongst the icy towers. Although he was the oldest and wisest whale, he liked to play with his family of whales, even though he was sleepy due to a large breakfast feast of small aquatic creatures moments before. As he tucked himself away from sight, he felt a strange sensation; his stomach seemed fuller than normal and it also had an odd rumbling sound emitting from it. What Barney didn't know was this....! As he had come up to the surface for air earlier, he had swallowed more than oxygen. As his gaping jaws opened on the surface, a rapidly moving coloured jigsaw piece swiftly moved past the black gaping hole of his jaws and into his digestive tract. As it came into contact with the water in this gullet, the mysterious but dormant jigsaw piece had had its magic ignited once again. The blue glow around the puzzle piece was reinstated; poised to grant the recipient's wish. Unbeknown to Barney, a most magical event was on the verge of happening. The mysterious jigsaw piece allowed one wish, the greatest heart-felt desire that any person could possibly want, and it would be granted in an instant. As a whale, Barney didn't really spend much of his time wishing for things that he didn't have; because he was a simple creature who was mostly content swimming around coral and wrecks. However, one of the oldest wrecks had a cabin that he often hid in. Upon the reverse of the door was a colourful poster of a place called Squidly Towers. Barney didn't know what this colourful picture represented; but he liked the variety of square shapes, curly lines linking these squares and strange symbols scribbled in different places. While Barney waited to be 'caught' he often studied the picture and wished that, maybe one day, he could visit such an exciting place. Barney's world was beautiful but unfortunately it was the same everywhere. Water, coral, plants, old metal and fishy friends.....and because of this he sometimes dreamt that he might visit somewhere a little different! (A bit like going on holiday for humans!) As he breathed in deeply to make himself significantly smaller to evade being caught, his tummy rumbled. A rumble so loud that the vast ship wreck shook! He looked down under his neck to check his elongated rubbery body and decided that is looked quite normal. He turned back to the picture once more and smiled a longing smile. The next thing he knew was some time later, when one of his school of whales shouted 'Boooooo' after finding his hiding place, startling Barney from his unexplainable daze.

The rides, shops and fun, put Barney in a flap!

A map, he stumbled upon a wonderful map.

CHAPTER 13

Dexter knew the way home. He had taken the same route many, many times. Across the park, along the winding river bank, over the stone bridge, turn left into the estate and his house was on the left. As remorseful as he felt about Dood's fate; it soon escaped his mind as he meandered half walking, half bunny hopping along with his nose stuck to the floor. Dexter loved sniffs! The stinkier the better too! The stinkiest sniffs were the only ones that stopped him entirely in his tracks, these often resulted in at least two loud woofs and the occasional full body roll! He was extremely careful that morning, not to sniff something so stinky that it made him sneeze! Magical adventures had been temporarily put on hold....and he was sure to maintain his stubborn stance!

As he steered left towards the bridge, with his nose stuck to the floor and waggy happy tail high in the air, he didn't take much notice of a white caddy van parked at the other side of the bridge. On the side of the van was a serious looking sign saying 'DOG WARDEN', but Dexter couldn't read so it didn't concern him in the slightest as he continued his sniffathon.

What perhaps should have concerned him was the man crouched down behind the large bush at the exit from the bridge with his large 'dog catcher net'. Obliviously, Dexter continued taking in his sniff adventure until he unknowingly walked straight into the large net trap, carefully positioned to catch him. Even though Dexter was in sniff heaven, he was quickly brought back to reality as he was swung over the man's shoulder, like a robber's swag bag and into the back of the white van. Feeling rather scared in the darkness of his new home, he looked around to see a cage surrounding him but the van was quite empty and bleak apart from himself. As Dexter didn't have his little Dood friend to help him out of his sticky situation, he wasn't quite sure what to do. "Errrr, what would clever Dood do just now...?" he thought to himself, with a little shake.

Seconds later the van began to move forwards on to a place unknown and Dexter started to feel scared. He gulped hard at the thought of being taken somewhere he didn't know. Helplessly he circled around his new cage looking for a way to escape but there was only the back door and a few windows; the cage also stopped him moving too far.   After five minutes of searching, his heart was beating fast in his chest; he sat down on the cold floor and began to have a little panic.

However, before he started to think about how he should panic, the van came to an unexpected halt!   He could hear the handbrake being clicked into a park position and the engine turned off.   "Quick Dexter think.....how can I get myself out of this sticky situation?" he thought to himself, cogs turning fast in his brain.   He laid his body on the cold floor, long and thin, with his head placed on his white paws (his best thinking position). The driver's door slammed shut and he heard the thud of heavy boots on the pavement as his captor walked towards the rear of the van.   He thought harder and harder but nothing sprung to his frightened mind.... the footsteps were getting closer.

"SNEEZE, a sneeze of course, a magnificent sneeze is what I need!" he suddenly thought, as if a bolt of lightning had struck him.   He closed his eyes, held his breath and sniffed.... But no sneeze came!   He sniffed the floor in desperation but still no sneeze...(it is rather tricky sneezing on command... try it sometime!). "Come on nose, don't fail me now," he thought, getting desperate.

The footsteps came to a halt outside the rear doors and Dexter could see the shadow of his captor outside through the windows. As one of the doors creaked open, Dexter started to think about his new life behind bars, eating tasteless left overs and he began to feel miserable. Gulping hard, Dexter looked up at the man dressed in black as the door revealed his face. Fortunately, as the cold air filled the inside of the van from outside, the change in temperature forced Dexter's dry sensitive nose to begin to twitch and seconds later he produced the noisiest sneeze! As he did, his ears and tail began to rotate, his nose began to light up with a strange glow and his loyal blue rockets replaced his paws. Expectantly, the captor in front of him, stood frozen to the floor with his mouth hung open. The man had never seen such a spectacle in his life! Moments later Dexter began to hover in the air, leaving his place of captivity behind. With a huge sigh of relief he headed for home as quick as he could, with no distractions.

Oh no! Look who is over the bridge.

It looks just like an almighty fridge.

CHAPTER 14

It was the coldest winter for many years, with snow falling for endless days causing the icebergs to grow taller and firmer. The coats of the Arctic animals had grown thicker as the biting wind blew and the sleet fell with force. Over the past few months life for Kasper had changed slightly for the better. After his new profession of fisherman had been refined, he had been able to feed himself daily, increasing his size back to its usual roundness.

As he had a coat of blubber under his fur, he had increased insulation from the coldness around him. He had learned how to swim and hold his breath for an increasing amount of time (unusual for a fur ball you are thinking). He had used his net to catch other finds from deep within the ocean. Due to his daily diet of fish and the increased amount of time spent in the sea, Kasper slowly started to evolve into a marine creature when he was in the water. Gills had started to form to help him breathe, his tail was fatter for propulsion in the water and his arms moved him swiftly through the water like fins. Incidentally he had also learned how to dive down to plunder the treasures from the shipwrecks below, all of which would be useful and needed for the future. Fortunately for Kasper he had a plan, a plan to firstly make his life comfortable once more, but secondly to see if his new skills could help him along the way to fulfil his long term goal of world domination.

Kasper had been very busy indeed, so busy in fact… that his luck was really beginning to change! The final icing on his cake was the home he had created for himself. Where on a desolate piece of ice could a ginger fur ball create a plush new pad? Under his iceberg is where! Whilst he had been diving down to the bottom of the ocean one day, he had become disorientated on his assent back up to the surface and had crashed into the base of the iceberg. Surprisingly, he realised that the inside of the iceberg was hollow and that the sea water didn't fill it (a bit like an air lock, it contained air that Kasper could breathe). Shocked he wandered in and couldn't believe his luck: a new hidden home for him. He had spent his time diving down to the wrecks on the ocean floor, picking treasures from below. He used wooden planks to make a floor just above the water level that he could then place his 'home' upon. Resourcefully he had dried out blankets and chairs to sit on, collected plates to eat off and even pinned the odd picture to the wall. As he wanted to connect himself with the world, just like humans, he had collected a strange box-like device from the helm of one of the boats. At first it looked like a telephone, but on closer inspection, he realised it was some sort of tracking device. When he switched it on, the screen had a series of green lines that were slight but constantly moving. When a fish swam past him in the water, he realised that a mark moved on the screen tracing the object below. This was going to take the place in his pad of the square box on the wall, in Old Rufus' home! Far more exciting he thought than Corporation Street or Westenders! Kasper was indeed proud of his new hidden pad.

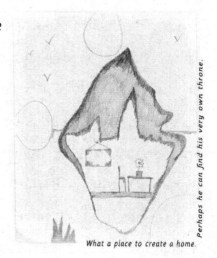

Perhaps he can find his very own throne.

What a place to create a home.

CHAPTER 15

Barney didn't know it just yet but his wish had been granted. As he had dozed in his hiding position, the puzzle piece had granted his greatest wish. Deep on the ocean floor an immense new world had been created. The finest three tier hotel, the fastest thrilling roller coasters, tasty eateries were all drilled into the ocean floor with non-meltable ice pillars. This city had not yet been discovered by Barney, as he was fast asleep in his usual home some metres away, exhausted from the hide and seek game the previous day.

That morning he had awoken before anyone else, feeling a little under the weather still. Reluctantly he swam off to stretch his fins and slowly swam to the surface of the ocean. He liked the fresh morning air and the brightness of the sun as it rose into the sky.   He took a deep breath through his blow hole, clearing out his lungs. As he took his final breath, the puzzle piece that had been left dormant rattling around his ample body, shot up high into the air as Barney ducked his body back below the surface of the water, heading towards his prize. Simultaneously the wise snowy owl who was about to head south for a winter break, swooped and picked up the puzzle piece in her beak and flew off into the distance. Deeper Barney headed through the water, his body heading in a direction that he hadn't swum to too many times before; he was unsure why but he enjoyed swimming at speed into the black unknown waters ahead.

In the right place at the right time.

The snowy owl with mighty wings soars and climbs.

CHAPTER 16

Dood had completed the science test, received his results, completed his detention to relearn the information that he neglected to learn first time round and then sat the test twice, in his own time, until he obtained the compulsory pass. Lesson learnt: it's better to do the work the first time round! But would he learn from this? Only time would tell!

It was Christmas time at Dood's house. His most favourite time of the year and Dexter's least favourite! The largest Christmas tree, that required at least half of the living room, replaced Dexter's toy box and Dood's Scalextric set and was decorated in ghastly pink bows, pink tinsel and pink flashing lights. Unfortunately Mum was a bit of a perfectionist with her tree and she spent hours placing bows in regular intervals, with baubles that hung in-between, so that it looked entirely symmetrical. Prior to this, Dad had had to bring his workmate and saw into the lounge to cut off various branches that either drooped the wrong way or had too many needles missing. This procedure took a long time, much to the dismay of Dood, as each year he brought his chocolate tree decorations out, eagerly awaiting the time he could place them on the tree but as yet, six years on, he was still waiting!

Usually this didn't bother Dood and Dexter, as they spent most of their time plotting magical adventures at the planning station under Dood's bed, in the room at the top of the house. However since their first and last magical disaster, Dexter had avoided talking about magic or adventure and had spent more of his time laid in front of the roaring fire in the lounge. Incidentally, Dood reluctantly spent increasing amounts of time sitting at the dining room table completing his homework or more favourably searching the internet for answers to the millions of questions he was asked by teachers, who should frankly already know the answers!

That Wednesday evening, school was about to finish for the holiday season, Dood walked home along his usual pathway, kicking snow into the air. It was freezing! Whilst a bracing wind forced him to increase his pace along the icy paths, he pulled his collar up around his ears and pushed his hands deeper into his pockets. As he was a few metres from home, he saw Dexter's tail sticking out from one of the bushes and expected Dexter to jump out on him as he walked closer. Cheerily, Dood decided that he would play the game too and ducked low behind the wall and crawled commando style stealthily towards his buddy. But Dexter didn't jump out, he didn't even walk - as Dood met his mate, he was sitting hiding with a rather forlorn look on his face.

"Hey buddy, what's up? Why are you sitting there?" Dood asked his friend, as best he could with the wind blowing a gale around him.

Dexter looked down, body slumped forward and his eyes began to fill with tears. "Dexter whatever is the matter? You never get upset... Has something happened at home?" he added as he fell to his knees in the snow beside Dexter, putting his hand on his ears tenderly. Sadly, Dexter started to shiver in the freezing temperatures. "Dexter....?" he stuttered, placing his arms around his buddy growing even more worried. Just as Dood was about to run home to get some help, Dexter lifted his head and jumped on his buddy licking his face, throwing snow all over Dood's cold body. "I got you...

One to me! Had you fooled!" Dexter mocked, jumping around in the snow, ears flapping.

Shocked, Dood had fallen back in the snow in surprise and his face indicated anger as well as frustration. Energetically Dood rose to his feet, dropped his school bag in the snow and picked up a pile of the freshest snow, forming a round snowball effectively in his palms. He expertly threw it at Dexter hitting him squarely on the nose, pushing his body backwards into the snow blanket. This activity continued for some time, much to the entertainment of the nosey neighbours with their pointy noses twitching behind their perfectly lined curtains. Even though Dood was angry with Dexter for the clever trick just moments before; he was extremely pleased to see his old buddy back to his playful self!

Since their fledgling adventure months before had almost wiped out the whole world, the 'real' Dexter had gone into hibernation. Behaviours such as sitting next to Mum in the lounge, curled up in his bed downstairs and an avoidance to talk about adventures had greatly worried Dood. (He even considered taking him to the vets but didn't know how he could explain the flying issue to Jane the vet). But the twinkle in Dexter's eye had certainly returned; he was back and that meant one thing.... ADVENTURE!

Strangely, the ice ball to the nose moments before had stunned Dexter and he shook his head like a propeller to reinstate his body parts to their rightful positions. And deep within his nose a sneeze was brewing.... He could feel it and he wasn't going to stop it! He was indeed ready for adventure! Looking on, Dood could see what was happening and the excitement inside him was evident! He jumped into the snow and completed a quick snow angel to celebrate as the vibrant blue rockets, shiny nose glow and propeller tail were evident once more.

Month after month, will they ever stall?

Grey clouds form and snow flakes fall.

CHAPTER 17

Gracefully the snowy owl flew away from the cold and ice that had frozen her nest. With the jigsaw piece held firmly in her beak, she was heading South where the sun made an appearance more frequently and warmed her feathers. She flew for hours and hours until her wings were so tired that she could fly no more. As she reached the warmer climes, she hovered above the luscious trees below, looking for somewhere to make her new nest and the puzzle piece in her beak would be her first addition.

Tired and weary she almost stopped.

A few more miles and then she flopped.

CHAPTER 18

Unsurprisingly Barney had never once looked back after stumbling upon his new home. When he saw the wonder in front of him that first day, his jaw, complete with four hundred spaced teeth, fell open at the spectacle before him. A sight welcomed him that was so magnificent and different to anything he had ever seen or eaten! It was also in stark contrast to the seaweed and coral that he glided through each day. The colour, the lights, the wooden signs, winding pebble paths, high slides and vast buildings were all whale sized and just so endearing to Barney and his family. Happily, Barney had grown quite fond of the oversized cushions in his new extravagant home; he had guppy servants available to serve the whole whale family, including sacks of krill cooked to their exact requirement. Barney's grandchildren enjoyed the spinning pods within the colourful gardens, whereas the parents preferred the thrill of rides; that pushed them at speed through the water, like a cork out of a bottle.

All of the structures, on closer inspection, had been formed with reinforced pillars drilled securely into the core of the Earth at the deepest part of the ocean. To house the largest mammals on planet Earth they had to be made of anti-melting ice towers with the strongest steel running through them.

Barney thought that he was the luckiest sea creature in the world and he often pondered where all this splendour had come from. His family had no need to venture far from their new home, as they had everything they needed, just as if their greatest aquatic wish had been granted!

Barney the whale, brave and strong.

He was so happy he broke into song.

CHAPTER 19

Rather than jumping excitedly onto Dexter's back and flying high into the wintery sky, Dood stopped himself. Whilst Dexter had been on 'sulking - I'm not doing anything until I sleep back my lost sleep' duty, Dood, when not pinned to the dining room table completing homework, had been busy upstairs in his own adventure station. Cleverly Dood knew that one day Dexter would be thirsty for adventure once more and he would be ready when he was. Ingeniously, he had spent his time creating refined 'mark 2' gadgets for his adventure belt and also many hours designing, creating and making their new superhero image!

Additionally, Dood had also decided that he needed to secure his room at the top of the house, from the crumblies and two girls that he lived with. He suspected that one day, a few months back, when he had foolishly left the door open as he left in a hurry, their room had been invaded by oldness and girliness....he had no evidence whatsoever, but he could smell that there had been an intrusion. Dood unfortunately for him, lived in a large house in the middle of an estate by the sea, with two girls named Sophie (bossy boots) and Olivia (precious princess) and the two crumblies - Mum and Dad.

Mum was a professional nagger and Dad spent his life under the bonnet of his white rally car in the garage next to the house. Dood could tolerate the crumblies as they fed him and allowed him to 'study' in his room. However, Granny was a different ball game altogether!

Dood and Granny had a temperamental love/hate relationship! She was the kindest Granny in the world despite the wart on the end of her nose and her constant "Doodle-doos" and tweaking of his cheeks when he greeted her. She was the Queen of embarrassing situations! Dood wasn't keen on being the centre of attention or being covered in lipstick but this seemed to happen to him more than both the girls put together! Chuckles of laughter from the girls also made the situation worse, as he was convinced they encouraged Granny to kiss him all the more!

Granny with her bright red lips.

Can you believe it? She can do the splits!

CHAPTER 20

Let us set the scene for the embarrassment torture that Granny excelled at.... One particular festive season, as the Christmas trees and lights went up in December, the boughs of holly decorated the halls, snow fell all about and the school nativity occurred! Dood was almost into juniors which meant that this year would be his last year of potential humiliation! Since joining school he had been lucky; the role of shepherd and innkeeper had been his previous starring roles and neither part had caused him too much trouble and the costumes were quite cool too. However, yearly there was always the risk of being given the lead role due to his name-sake! And where there was stardom, there was potential for forgetting the lines or even worse Granny making him an elaborate costume fit for such a Hollywood role!

As the names were announced this particular year, Dood waited with baited breath for the role that he would be given this frosty winter. Under his breath he kept repeating, "Not Joseph, any role but Joseph please!" as Mary was announced, followed by the donkey, camels, kings and mushrooms (it was one of those modern nativities) and Dood's name had not been mentioned. Foolishly, he almost began to think that they had forgotten to give him a role and he could perhaps shift the scenery on stage instead! He was about to complete a little celebratory chuckle when the final two roles were announced, ".....and the role of Jesus' father Joseph goes to......Herbert Hinchcliff!" A loud applause erupted as Herbie blushed and bowed to the cheering teachers and children, "and finally the last important role goes to Joseph Redford, who this year will be a ....present, a sparkly, pink present!"

Suddenly, Dood thought his hearing was playing tricks on him and even perhaps that he was dreaming. But no, sure enough he was going to take the place of a pink present in front of hundreds of people. How would he cope with the humiliation? The girls in his class thought that a pink present would be just the coolest thing, however the boys put aside their own embarrassment of tea-towels and dressing gowns and even dresses for a sparkly pink present! Oh the shame!

As Dood had walked home that evening he had decided that he needed to execute two key events to ensure that he had any credibility left. He needed to lose the slip that asked parents to make the costumes and bring them in by the following Monday and also the ticket request letter, asking parents if they wanted to watch the play. He knew the exact place he would lose them; the bin in the park. So a slight detour home and the disaster was averted. However when Granny arrived for tea the following day, not only did she have the money in her hand for a front row ticket, she had also meandered down to the local electrical shop, found the largest box known to man and had spent the day decorating it with pink. Disheartened, Dood also realised that Mum had an additional bag of pinkness to add and the two of them spent an hour admiring the present that had been created! I bet you are wondering how they knew? Dood definitely wondered - The school had just signed up to a new text messaging service, hence the information had got through!

Rehearsals or torture, depends how you saw it, unfolded a whole new level of embarrassment for Dood. Sadly, he wasn't in the first scene, nor the second or even straight after the break....no he was the finale, the last memory that all of the audience would go away with... ingrained in their memories forever! Dood had to jump out of the present and give the Headteacher Miss Snitch a gift from the school and start the singing of 'We wish you a Merry Christmas.' Rather ashamed, he began to think that playing Joseph would have been a far better deal.

The evening of the performance arrived, obviously Dood tried his usual faking illness, limb falling off and various other ways to stop the torture that was about to happen. However, Mum wasn't the most sympathetic creature (she was used to such Oscar winning acting performances from Dood and Dexter) and he was scooped up and directed towards the car, present in the boot - with extra pinkness added due to apparent 'falling off' of so many pink accessories during rehearsals.

Surprisingly the performance went swimmingly and no one forgot their lines, sheep or presents and baby Jesus was delivered safely into the world once more. Sadly, Granny and Mum were both in the front row of the audience, only metres away from the stage.

As the end of the performance drew closer, the present with Dood hiding inside, was placed on the stage. After the final applause Dood waited for his moment, Miss Snitch got up and was about to speak...."3...2....1.....and go!" Up he shot, like a cork from a bottle, which he had rehearsed a million times before.   Unfortunately Miss Snitch in her skyscraper heels (these only came out for important events) was perched on the fragile lid of the present where his head and body were supposed to pop out through, speaking to the enthralled audience. With a thud, immediately Dood realised that his exit out was blocked, as he tried to push it with all his might! What he didn't realise (nor Miss Snitch) was that the top lid of the box was flimsily wrapped, to make the present look more present-like, and to allow Dood to break through it and as Snitch's body weight transferred to her bottom as she sat, she started to fall through the present onto the waiting Dood.

Resourcefully Dood tried to push her back up, but she was too heavy and gravity helped pull her downwards. As quick as a flash, Granny and Mum jumped out of their premium front row seats and grabbed a foot each to try to spare Snitch's embarrassment and a squashed Dood. Muffled giggles from the audience could be heard as they believed this was the finale to the show. Finally a comical tug-of-war scene unfolded until the sides of the box split and everyone landed in a great heap on the stage to a standing ovation. Half squashed, half relieved and flushed with embarrassment Dood stood up and bowed; he was just thankful the whole experience was over and Gran, Mum and Snitch brushed themselves off as they appeared unharmed. Just as Dood thought he had had a lucky escape, Granny walked over to him and gave him the biggest, reddest, wettest kiss she had ever delivered in front of his whole school. With a complexion to match any pillar box, Dood walked off the stage, hopeful that the audience would remember the comedy of the box split, rather than the kiss of 'doom!'

However this present created a monumental stink!

Pink, precious, sparkly pink.

CHAPTER 21

After the potential room invasion, Dood had concluded that he must secure his room in the most effective way specifically to keep out girls more than crumblies, and to do so he had to think creatively. The water bomb suspended from the ceiling outside his doorway had failed him! He was so sure that he had been invaded by girls (this was the worst thing imaginable in the whole world) and had to be prevented from ever happening again. What if they had stumbled upon his superhero gadgets or plans?....the thought was unimaginable! He needed something more preventative and obvious, so that they wouldn't dare set foot onto the top tier of the house. Carefully he rummaged under his bed for his army cargo net, used when he was going through a 'soldier' phase! But it wasn't there. He tried the back of his closet, top of his wardrobe and still no luck, however he finally found it down the back of the radiator, this he recalled proved the most efficient hiding place (just a shame he had forgotten that he had placed it there - so that proved its success as a hiding place, he thought!).

Quickly, he pulled off the fluff, cobwebs and sausage roll remains and spread it out squarely on his bedroom floor. Next he placed metal hooks on each of the corners of the net; this was the easiest part..... the tricky part followed. Sneakily he needed to borrow the step ladders from the cupboard next door to the crumblies' room, climb up and then screw the hooks into the ceiling in the correct places to ensure that the netting would lay flat. As a novice superhero, he surprisingly managed this section of his plan with ease, however just as he was securing the last screw, Sophie (the nosiest sister) came poking about upstairs. Dood was suspended at the very highest section of the ladder when he spotted her on the prowl. To avoid potential rumbling, he kicked the ladder so that it fell silently onto the bed in his room and he precariously held onto the hooks in the ceiling, a bit like Spider-Man! Sophie, like a sophisticated cat burglar, walked up the stairs slowly checking around each corner. Her breathing was laboured as she finally reached the outside of Dood's room. From above, Dood was growing crosser and crosser and was about to jump down on top of her, when Dexter came bounding up the staircase. Unfortunately, Sophie must have heard his claws tapping on the floor in the hall and very quickly ran back down the stairs to her room and slammed the door behind her, evading capture.

Bounding with energy, Dexter ran into their room and looked around for his friend. "I'm up here buddy!" Dood whispered careful not to rouse Sophie's attention once more. Ears firmly forward for maximum listening, Dexter looked around... Under the bed, in the planning station and out of the window... But Dood was nowhere to be seen! Dood's room was the only room at the top of the house and so he couldn't be anywhere else!

"I'm above your head Dexter, look up," Dood whispered as loud as he could, with strain and pain in his voice from the hanging position above him. Immediately, Dexter planted his bottom on the floor directly under his little buddy. "That is amazing Dood, what are you doing up there? Are you thinking about us moving our room into an upside down position so that we can hide away from the world of nosiness?" Dexter mocked from below.

"Noooo!" Dood shouted through gritted teeth! "I am attaching this net so that we can drop it on suspicious looking snoopers! I've just caught one of them sneaking up on us moments before. If you hadn't disturbed her, I think she would have snooped around to her heart's content! Imagine that eh buddy.. She might have found all of my new adventure secrets...!"

Worried, Dexter asked, "What adventure secrets?...I don't remember anything new the last time I was in here!"

"I'll explain in a minute, can you please help me down..? My arms are going to fall off!" Dood shouted in exasperation.

As if he was jolted back into thinking mode, Dexter ran into the bedroom and pulled a small blue cushion, the size of a comic, off the bed between his gnashers and placed it directly under Dood. Desperately, Dood was red in the face by now and could not hold his body weight a moment longer. He looked down just in time, hopeful that his buddy had brought something large and soft from his room like a mattress or mini trampoline to break his fall. The sight of the tiny cushion took the breath from his lungs, as he fell like a heap of logs onto the hard wooden floor. Unbelievably, the cushion hadn't broken his fall!

Flat on his back, stars circling above his head. Dexter ran over and licked his friend's face! "Didn't I do well, that cushion was a fabulous idea - one of my best I think!" he explained, pleased as punch with himself!

Temporarily unable to speak due to the impact of the fall, the glare that Dood gave Dexter told him that his buddy didn't quite agree with his choice of 'breaking falls' materials! Moments later, that seemed like years to Dex, Dood got his breath back and looked straight at his furry friend who was now sitting facing him only centimetres away, with his most sorrowful look on his face! "It's ok Dexter, just try to use that fine brain of yours. A cushion with this much stuffing will not help me, will it!" he relented pointing to the pitiful cushion.

"I'm sorry, but aren't you pleased I tried... we all have to start somewhere with using our common sense and you know that dogs aren't gifted in such a way!" Dexter tried to explain. Even though Dexter was a brave and courageous puppy he often needed his friend to help him with decisions from the human world - he was trying to understand the strange race of humans he lived with and encountered daily - dog behaviour is much simpler he felt and humans could learn from this! But he wasn't going to get into a conversation about this right now!

Downstairs they heard the crumblies and girls slam the front door shut and the car engine roared. Relieved, they knew they had a short undisturbed moment to attach the release strings to the hooks and then add the mini water bombs, stink bombs and bath bombs to the net for extra security. Together they worked as a well-oiled machine and within an hour they stood back, hands on hips and paws in the air to admire their handiwork - No one was going to get past this advanced security operation. Any foolish intruder who walked into their room, would trip over the wire that releases the net - ingenious!

Just like Spiderman, Dood hung from the roof.

Look up Sophie, you can see the proof.

CHAPTER 22

School, thankfully, was closed for a few weeks, Dexter was back to himself and the crumblies and girls were distracted with movie watching and wrapping things in coloured paper! That meant one thing! The time was right to practise their 'flying' and superhero techniques so that they could become the world's greatest superhero team... Forget Superman and Captain America! They were going to put those guys to shame - aiming high, well maybe a bit too high, was where Dood wanted to be and nothing was going to stop him!

Secure in the knowledge that they were protected from nosiness, Dood shut his bedroom door and sat around his adventure planning station with Dexter, situated under his bed. Careful not to blurt out all of fabulous plans at once, Dood took a deep breath and started to explain to Dexter all the planning that he had been perfecting whilst he was sleep recovering (sulking). "Right Dood. Firstly we need to perfect our flying and landing... But secondly, I wanted to show you some of the new tools that I have created to capture criminals and..." lowering his voice to almost a whisper, "and show you our new superhero, crime fighting costumes!"

"I've spent a lot of time thinking about our flying and I think we need to go to...." Dexter started, "What did you say...costumes?! You know my feelings on costumes Dood, I refuse to become a laughing stock of the puppy community again... I've only just regained my credibility since the last time! So no chance... It's fur or NO adventure! Your choice buddy!"

"Wait till you see them first... I've made modifications that will give you amazing street credibility. Every puppy on the block will want one..!" Dood retaliated, wagging his pointy finger in a convincing, explaining way in front of Dexter.

The expression of sulkiness was beginning to develop on Dexter's face. Enthusiastically, Dood ran to his pine wardrobe placed adjacent to his bed and stood diligently next to it like a proud parent. He held onto the handle, took a deep breath and explained, "Let me show you first, before you get into a strop!" Dishearteningly, Dexter huffed a bored sigh, rolled his oval brown eyes and laid down on his stomach with head on his outstretched paws.

As enthusiastically as a nine year old girl slipping on her first pair of heels, Dood shouted, "Right boys and girls.... Give a loud drum roll for the world's greatest superheroes of all time.... Dexter and Dood..." and simultaneously he opened both wardrobe doors with pride, to present his prize inside. Placed with care, on the back of the doors were two blue costumes suspended on black hangers: one dog size and one boy sized.

"Nope, they are awful," Dexter stubbornly retorted, staring at the floor without even looking at them, "I'm not wearing that!" and he stood, turned on his paws, tail waving crossly in the air and started to walk towards the exit.

"Hang on a minute; I've spent ages making these... Let me explain!" Dood pleaded, running around his sulky friend, standing firm with his hands on his hips, blocking the way out. Dexter reluctantly stopped in his tracks.

"Look Dex..." he welcomed, "I have created yours so that the blue section that goes round your body is exactly the same as the red coat that you like to wear..." Dood explained, to a slightly more interested Dexter. "The cape is small, almost not there at all, as last time it kept flapping in my eyes and isn't made of that slippy material that caused loads of disasters! Also your mask has been changed to a hat that goes over your ears and eyes and so won't slip down in front of your face. Finally the section that you moaned the most about, the golden D to identify us, is absolutely tiny on your cape and is not sparkly in anyway!" Dood concluded with a satisfied smile.

"....I can tell you have been very busy whilst I've been sleeping Dood. I guess slightly more to a dog's tastes than the first model, but I can't have a hat over my ears as they are my handle bars aren't they? You won't be able to steer with them if they are squashed into a hat," Dexter questioned with interest, but continued to put 'blocks' in Dood's way!

Eyes full of enthusiasm as Dexter seemed to be taking this much better than expected, "I've thought of that one too..." he exclaimed, jumping into the air, "I've cut out ear shapes holes in the hat that will allow your ears to be moved but will keep the rest of your head toasty warm... Ingenious!" he shouted pleased as punch with himself.

Dexter wanted to stand there and hate the whole costume, as he just wanted to be a cute furry dog. Dressing up was not his favourite pass time - that was for giggly girls who liked fluff and sparkle. But he had to relent, he really liked the costume and he thought so would his fans and most importantly the dogs on his patch! "Er... I guess I could have a little try on and see how it looks," Dexter reluctantly offered. Dood could tell that his best buddy was pulling his leg with his negative attitude and knew he was secretly onto a winner; his heart jumped with excitement.

Quickly Dood pulled his own costume off the back of the door, which was exactly the same as the last model apart from it wasn't made from the horrible silky material that caused Dood to spend most of his time hanging upside down around Dexter's rounded tummy. Consequently the golden D on the back of his cloak was much larger than last time, to compensate for the smaller version on Dexter's back. The world, after all, needed to be able to recognise them... he didn't want them to get confused with other such pretend feeble heroes!

Equipped for adventure, they were about to walk out of their door, when Dood remembered about all of his new inventions that he had made to fit into his adventure belt. "Hang on Dexter, look at these little beauties that I have created!" he offered, holding out a box with 'KEEP OUT' written across the side that he slid out from the hiding place on top of his wardrobe.

As he was now a more informed adventurer, Dood had realised that he needed to make retrieval devices for differing situations such as space, water, land and heat etc to ensure his belt was equipped for every situation. Consequently, to add to his trusty catapult and extendable grabbers, Dood had modified his snorkel set to ensure they could breathe under water if needed. With the stealth of a secret agent, he 'borrowed' Mum's oven gloves and changed them slightly to make a heat resistant shield and finally he had used Dad's hose pipe to make a complex breathing device for toxic and watery situations. Impressed, Dexter took in every moment of the explanation and watched Dood place them into his adventurer's belt that snap-locked around his narrow waist. Finally, they were ready to start their training... and even more excitedly their next adventure. Dood was so excited; he could almost burst.

Impatiently, the duo headed for the bedroom door and began to walk down the stairs, being sure to avoid nosy or annoying people. (Panic not: it was dark outside and that was the only reason that Dexter was agreeable with going outside in his neighbourhood wearing fancy dress).

Dexter, the only superhero who hates dressing up.

CHAPTER 23

Kasper K.Itty was an evil cat. He had spent the majority of his adult kitty years planning and plotting how he could rid the world of humans as well as ruling planet Earth his way. An Earth where animals ruled, cats reigned supremely and there were no ridiculous rules that needed to be followed like bin emptying on Tuesday, money having to be stored in banks and driving on the right hand side of the road.

Even though Kasper had lost all his luxury, splendour and magic that the puzzle piece had provided him; he was more determined than ever to gain world domination - 'I'll show them... who needs stupid magic?' was his motto. For sometime he believed his luck had run out when he almost drowned in the iciest water he had ever experienced but now things were looking a little brighter. Over time, as Kasper ate more fish and spent more of his time in the deep ocean, his features became even more nautical. The majority of his time was spent exploring the ocean floor below and he found the colour and the diversity of the ocean creatures simply fascinating. Ingeniously he copied their swimming techniques and refined his ability to catch small fish to eat. He even found an old, oval glass bowl in one of the shipwrecks and caught himself a couple of small fish to keep as pets, Meg and Mog, in his ice home under the iceberg.

More importantly Kasper had started to form a plan in his mind, a most clever and calculating plan, but before he could finalise his ideas he needed to find a few vital ingredients. His plan was ignited by a book he found aboard one of the wrecks that had cabins inside. Under one of the beds he discovered a book called 'The Earth - A Simple Guide for Beginners' which he found rather informative. Inside the central pages was a coloured picture that he had studied for many hours. Interestingly the illustration was a cross section of the Earth: the mantle, crust and core and how they all laid on top of each other like the layers of an onion. It was the fiery molten liquid, squashed in the centre deep below the crust (the top section that we walk on and grow plants on; like a pie crust) and the hard inner core (the ball of solid rock right in the middle of the Earth) that amazed Kasper. "How can there be funny, runny liquid, like honey, so hot, fiery and dangerous squirming about under where I swim?" he often wondered to himself when the ocean felt so cold to him.

To add extra interest to his wonder about what was below his feet (fins); there was a large crack in a section of the ocean floor, exposing some of the crust below. On occasions he and many other sea creatures swam over this crack. There was a jet of warm and sometimes very hot water that squirted out from this crack and the creatures of the ocean welcomed the warmth that it gave and were often seen basking in the jets - a bit like a shower! (No Radox shower gel though!) Strangely, Kasper's book explained what this was but the words were too long for him to read.... 'geo something and the word spring' was its reference in his book but he knew that springs were used in pogo sticks, so he thought the book was a bit inaccurate at times. But it did explain that the water was heated from the boiling liquid below and he loved the heat that it provided. Finally the boring pages of the book that Kasper often skipped through, but he still liked the pictures, explained how this boiling core kept planet Earth stable and warm, a bit like the roaring fire on a cold day in Old Rufus' house and how without it - planet Earth could shrink, how land could disappear below water, or how it could potentially freeze over or even end up as a tired, useless piece of rock!

All of this extensive reading had triggered the wicked cogs to turn once more in Kasper's mind. If this core thing was so important in maintaining planet Earth as it is, then maybe there was the most perfect opportunity to cause a little mayhem and panic above. All Kasper needed to learn now, was how to get access to the molten liquid below the surface and how he could begin to cool this core down. Now there was a plan, but where to start without magic was going to cause a few problems but Kasper was determined to find a way.

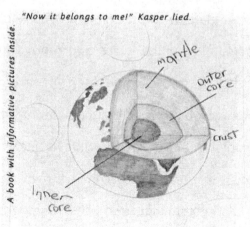

"Now it belongs to me!" Kasper lied.

A book with informative pictures inside.

mantle

outer core

crust

inner core

CHAPTER 24

Barney the whale loved the luxury in which he lived. He took the role of wise Granddad to his own family but also to many of the other creatures of the ocean. As the kindest most giving creature, his warmth had extended to many groups of ocean creatures. Cleverly and kindly, he had created a developing city where creatures lived contentedly together, sharing his fortune from the puzzle piece with many others. Over time, the splendour that he had received had spread widely across the sea bed welcoming creatures great and small, the space had evolved to be specific to the diversity and needs of those that lived there.

Currently a family of lobsters were busy building a new lobster house, next door to where the crabs had created their home complete with garden and tree house for the young nippers. Dolphins were rearranging a pile of irregular rocks to make some kind of exercise yard. Clown fish in aprons ran one of the many restaurants and were cooking on a rocky stove a feast for some visiting jellyfish in their eatery called Clown Cuisine. At the far side of the colourful and busy town was a family of sharks who were using a drill and a digger to excavate a site, possibly looking for buried treasure or digging footings for a stunning vibrant building. Central to the city was a rustic old church where Willow the ray fish was the resident minister and the main local shop was Chucklebury's run by the Arctic cod family.

Sharks with muscles and very sharp teeth.

Be sure to avoid the beautiful coral reef.

CHAPTER 25

Outside in the snow and ice, Dexter and Dood ran along the path towards the woods, their favourite place in the world. Like the wind, Dexter charged along, nose down and tail flat whilst Dood held firmly onto the end of his green lead 'flying' behind. Fresh snow had started to fall which made them even giddier, as they followed the winding paths up to the flattest part of the woods where the trees had been felled this past Autumn. Resourcefully Dood had placed a torch on his head and led the way through the light it emitted. On several occasions Dexter abruptly halted his four paw drive in mid run and they skidded out of control on the ice, like a toboggan! "Oh Dexter I'm so glad you are back to your amazing self... I was getting a bit worried a few weeks back that I had lost my best friend forever!" he panted as he flew, enjoying the speckles of snow hitting his face like a pin ball machine.

Panting, ears flapping and tongue tossing side to side in excitement, Dexter answered, "Didn't it scare you though Dood, if we hadn't involved ourselves - we would all be in puppy heaven right now? I would have preferred to leave the rescuing to the people who wear uniform and have flashing lights attached to their cars... they are more suitably trained than us!"

Dood paused and thought a minute, "I agree Dex, but we said that we would have a little practise and then try simple rescues especially at this time of the year, with people slipping all over the place... What's the harm in that?"

"Defo' Dood! I feel torn, as I do feel blessed to have special powers which I think most folk would love to have and I should use them wisely but I just get a bit scared that that pesky cat is still somewhere doing something horrible. I wish he was behind bars right now, I think I would sleep much better knowing that Dood!" Dexter surmised, with such responsibility.

Hopeful and confidently, Dood answered, "Well all the more reason to make sure we are ready if he ever dares to rear his frightful face, I say."

Panting, the duo reached their destination point. "This torch is hurting my head Dexter, can you illuminate your nose so that I can take it off?" Dood asked, fiddling with the elastic around his head. As Dood turned round,

Dexter had disappeared. Patiently Dood used the torch to look around the immediate area and began to have a little panic in the dark. Dood didn't have to look far, Dexter was deep in the fresh snow amongst the undergrowth shovelling the fresh white flakes with his nose, sniffing for new smells. "Dex! Come on buddy!" he shouted exasperated. But Dex was in sniff heaven. The snow made the smells much more intense and he loved having a pile of white fresh snow on the end of his nose; it kept it cold and wet, just the way he liked it!

Relieved that he knew where his buddy was, Dood used the light on his head to arrange some of the logs and boulders that had been discarded amongst the felling. Carefully he rolled them into position so that the boulder was deep under a collection of logs, to create a person stuck under a pile of debris. Pleased with his handiwork for such a little person, he placed his hands on his hips to observe his assimilated scene. Dexter by now, had a rather wet head from shovelling all of the snow on his nose, but was excited about his sniff collection and most importantly could feel a sneeze coming on, with all of the snow inhalation.

Slowly, Dexter emerged from the undergrowth and stood still, four paws equally spaced, knees slightly bent gripping the slippy surface; a full head shake followed with ears flapping, jowls emitting jowl juice all over the floor and surrounding plants. Amusingly, he then stuck his bottom in the air, tail so high it looked like an antennae and lowered his front paws so that they were flat on the ice; he looked ready to pounce but he was waiting for something far more magical. Three....two..... he started to inhale, eyes closed, braced himself for impact.... one.... he sneezed so loud that the creatures who were hibernating were sure to have been disturbed from their extended slumber. Eyes wide open Dood stood back to watch; he enjoyed watching the magic take hold more than anything else in the world.

Rapidly Dexter's nose lit up with a warm glow, his white and ginger tail began to spin, blue rockets appeared where his paws stood moments previously and his pouch containing blue magical dust reappeared, fur coloured, parallel with his chin upon his white and ginger chest. Expertly, Dexter started to hover just above the ice, facing his buddy ready for lift off.

Eager to be flying once more, Dood swung his leg over Dexter's back standing on tip toes and Dexter kindly lowered himself as low to the ground as he could. Once aboard, Dood smugly thought about how different the fabric choice of their costumes felt; he was much more secure sitting upon his back, hands on his ears ready to steer the handlebars. "Right the plan is as follows: I'm going to turn off my light and you are going to use your nose to light the way....the problem is ahead of us, a child (the boulder) is stuck under a pile of logs and we are going to fly over, rescue her and then fly off, waving to the public as we go...!" Dood explained, once again getting carried away with himself.

"Ha ha! Do you think we should try to refine the flying first rather than worrying about the public Dood! Our last altercations made the public quite frightened with our disasters rather than rescues, so I think we should focus on that first!" Dexter suggested, trying to calm Dood down a little.

"Dex you can be such a party-pooper sometimes.... I'm just so excited to be back... I do wonder if our fans have been worried about our whereabouts for the past few months!" he continued in a daze!

"Yes, can't you see the crowds just behind those trees over there Dood, we'll need security before we know it!" Dexter answered sarcastically, pointing into the trees. Ignorantly, Dood ignored his jibes and continued with his plan.

"Right where is the direction dial?" Dood questioned, searching about Dexter's neck where the dial once grew. It was still there but slightly higher than before and this time it had 'the most simple dial ever made for dogs' written around the furry dial in a circle. Shocked, Dood was quite offended by this but secretly hoped it was much simpler to direct the flying direction, as he was the poorest navigator first time round. This time it had four arrows, each a basic primary colour, pointing to the four directions of the compass. Covering the dial was a transparent plastic cover, in red letters it said 'FOR EMERGENCIES (and there will be!), press this button firmly and flying will immediately STOP! Secretly Dood's pride was beginning to take a knock. He and Dexter were going to be amazing superheroes, not at all like this dial believed them to be - a duo of bumbling buffoons!

Determined to get it right! Dood sitting upright, back straight, held onto the left steering device (ear) with his left hand and with his right hand tentatively pressed the 'up' direction button carefully. Expecting to go downwards, he braced for impact but rather surprisingly Dexter began to hover ever so slightly off the floor. He placed his right hand on Dexter's right ear and maintained a safe hover until they were about ten metres off the ground. Overwhelming pleased with himself, Dood released his hand once more and pressed the right button, tugged Dexter's ear again to the right and like an experienced driver beyond his years, he turned towards the 'catastrophe' in front of them.

As they hovered closer to the 'action', Dood took out his 'Indiana Jones' whip from his adventurer's belt and forcefully aimed for the log, curled the whip securely around the thickest section and then placed Dexter in reverse going left rather than right and within five minutes the 'victim' had been returned to safety. Not one jot of a problem, not even a sniff! A bystander would have thought that they had been professional superheroes all of their lives. Not a word was exchanged between the two as they executed their perfect rescue, no sharp breaths and no 'look outs!' for the first time ever!

Safely, Dood landed Dexter and the two of them completed a little celebration woof and dance!

"Words cannot describe how amazing that flying experience was Dexter! You are positively an expert! I would quite happily let the whole world know about our brilliance right now! I just knew we could do it Dex!" he bragged, pride beaming from him as he stroked Dexter's head in reward.

"It certainly was a very different experience to the last flying experiment we had Dood! Maybe you are right, maybe we could be amazing!" he half hoped that his thoughts were true.

They were ready for real adventure and the confidence the two felt as they walked back home was as high as the highest skyscraper! What could possibly go wrong?

Flying through the trees and bushes.

Up, down and round the duo rushes.

CHAPTER 26

Hidden from view Kasper had stumbled upon Barney's vibrant city. Patiently, he camped out day and night behind a section of coral on the outskirts of the city and watched and waited, waited and watched. Frequently he had to return to the surface of the water for air, as he was still unable to remain under water for extended periods.

Usefully, he had found a black rock that he could scratch his notes into with a sharp piece of shell he'd polished into a pencil shape. He was especially interested in the machinery used to drill holes into the ocean floor, how these were operated and where they were stored. He was also extremely intrigued about the pillars used for the foundations of the extensive buildings across the city: Why didn't these melt when they were drilled deep into the floor and beyond? Kasper had so many questions and as he wrote his notes and observed the activities of the creatures, some of his queries were answered. But whilst a cat, who had reluctantly learnt the art of patience, sat waiting; the foundations of his evil plan were forming and very soon he would execute phase one and bring about complete chaos to the Earthlings above and he could not wait to see the product of his hard work.

A clever and evil plan unfolds.

CHAPTER 27

After his lengthy wait, Kasper excitedly returned to his iceberg home and sat at the table, made by himself from reclaimed wood he had found floating in the ocean. Three chairs were placed under the table; each one different, as they were collected from various ship wrecks on the ocean floor. Cleverly, he had stumbled upon his own perfect writing tool in the form of slate, mud that had been squashed under coral and rocks over millions of years. Using shells that he sharpened to make pencils, he was able to record his thoughts and ideas (Kasper unfortunately had a poor memory) but arrogantly believed that when he held world domination, creatures may delight in finding his plans of destruction years in the future.

Parts of the old Kasper were beginning to rear themselves. He had managed to 'convince' a dopey octopus called Oswald and Edmund the scatty elephant seal to be his willing servants within his ice home and strangely they seemed keen to support Kasper in any way they could (perhaps they liked the plush cushions and cooked fish that Kasper was providing 'free' for them). This enabled Kasper to stay in his home planning and plotting whilst he had two willing gophers to go and collect or look at something for him; ensuring his time was far more productively spent on more life changing events! As he sent his workers off to calculate how deep into the ocean's floor the mechanical drill on the building site in Barney's city would go; Kasper completed his master plan upon his slate.

To summarise: Kasper's plan involved using the non-meltable ice pillars that formed the foundations of all of the vast buildings and he was going to drill them through the ocean floor and into the boiling molten liquid that kept the planet stable and warm, causing the heated lava to cool and eventually freeze. Similarly to months before when he had almost completed world domination, he knew that when his plan was executed to perfection, the changes on Earth would be slow and progressive but dramatic enough to make people panic and then finally he would increase his meddling until BOOM! Earth as all the Earthlings knew it would be no more... and more importantly his destruction could not be reversed! (Old man Rufus, Kasper's former faithful owner, had reversed all of his handiwork last time and Kasper was going to make certain that history wouldn't repeat itself).

They are eager to please, support the needy and help them heal.

Ozzy octopus and Ed the elephant seal.

Let us introduce you to:

CHAPTER 28

In a tired, ramshackle house in the middle of an evergreen wood, an old man lay snoozing in his threadbare chair, beside a roaring open fire. Eerily, the house stood alone in its own grounds that were overgrown and unkempt. The nearest neighbours were many miles away in the next small village. Old Rufus Rule was an old man! He was so old that he forgot what day it was, he couldn't remember which day he went shopping nor which day his bin was collected. He was a scatty, kind old man with fluffy white hair, who wore his glasses on the end of his nose and wore washed-out dungarees, complete with patches on the knees.

This is how Rufus appeared to the outside world. He was old, possibly double the age of any other living human and found moving difficult unless a dangerous situation occurred and then he was as sprightly as a ten year old!

Old Rufus was a mysterious and intriguing man and no one really knew him at all (and this is the way he liked it!). He had, previously, been the Protector of the Puzzle Piece of Divine Creation (You know....the one we saw float through the atmosphere into Barney's tummy!). For many years before this time, it had been kept safe from harm through three generations until his pet cat had stolen it. That pet cat was called Kasper K.Itty and he had once been a cute, orange fluff ball who purred for his misshapen biscuits and cat milk. However, Rufus' first, hugest, mistake to date was letting Kasper into his cellar where the puzzle piece was held and his second monumental error was sharing the mystery of its powers with him. Months later Kasper had stolen it and unfortunately knew exactly how to grant his inner wishes and this is how Earth came under threat for the first time in its history: and Rufus blamed himself entirely for that.

Even though Rufus did not know exactly where the puzzle piece was in the world; one of the many mysteries surrounding Rufus was that he just seemed to know whether it was safe or not - a bit like a sixth sense.

As old people do, Rufus had his routines. He only left the house once a week to do his shopping at the local store and he went on the same day, at the same time, and was gone for exactly one hour, not a minute longer.

Also, Rufus liked to potter in his overgrown garden at the rear of his house, not to complete the weeding and digging that so desperately needed doing, but to venture into the small derelict wooden hut at the very end of his two acres of land. This hut housed a variety of birds, mostly owls that came to visit from time to time. Rufus enjoyed talking to his visiting animals and he fed them, gave them a comfortable bed and kept them warm in the biting temperatures.

Lately he had spent more of his time in this hut as he was awaiting the arrival of the snowy owls that came for their winter holidays, to protect them from the icy climes of the Arctic, but as yet they had not visited. Old Rufus was a patient man and he sat on his rickety stool in the hut and scrutinised the greying sky, eagerly awaiting his next visitors.

Forgetful, old, decrepit but kind.

If you dig a bit deeper - what would you find?

CHAPTER 29

With new found confidence, Dood and Dexter slept more soundly than they had done for months that night. Dood at the top of his cabin bed, dressed in his superhero onesie, wrapped in thick duvet and Dexter lay beside him, stretched out on his back - four legs pointing towards the ceiling. Similarly, the duo were having the same amazing dream... they were flying through the towering buildings after a 'bad' man on an ice cloud. As that villain turned to them, they both jumped in their sleep as they realised that that man wasn't a man, it was a dastardly feline that they had become very familiar with months before - Kasper K.Itty! Unfortunately, the dream progressed, in a frightening manner, as the chase wove them through the towering buildings and expelled them into the greying ocean where the kitty hunted them with an icy bullet from a monstrous cannon, which was executed with precision causing them to fall into the freezing ocean below! Both Dood and Dexter woke with a sudden start, sitting bolt upright in unison.

Panting, "Buddy, I just had the worst dream ever! We were flying through the city and.." Dood blurted out at speed stumbling over his words, sweat pouring from brow, expression flushed and panicked.

Eyes as wide as saucers, Dexter interrupted, "Me too...I can't believe that evil pesky cat is still flying about in my dreams. But Dood.." he gasped sharply, "I told you, don't you remember, that whilst I was sleeping my lost sleep back that I kept having this awful feeling that he was still around, plotting and planning, I just knew it!"

"Look Dexter, let's not over dramatise things here, it just might be a coincidence. We feel more confident about our flying and rescuing techniques and this possibly triggers something in our dreams... nothing more, nothing less," Dood rationalised, but secretly he was also thinking the same thing at the back of his mind.

"The other thing that concerned me greatly is the water that we had to fly over... You know my issue with water Dood, that worried me more than the fur ball!" Dexter answered, shaking slightly as he spoke.

Sympathetically, Dood leant forwards towards his frightened friend, "Don't worry Dex, I am fully aware of your fear of water and don't worry, none of our adventures will go anywhere near the soggy stuff!"

When Dexter was an adorable puppy, he had ventured round to Granny's with the family. In Granny's garden was a pond, complete with various sized goldfish and a noisy toad family. As inquisitive puppies do; he meandered down to the water and thought it was a large drinking bowl, similar to his own in the house. As he bent down under the safety wire, balancing on the stones that enclosed the pond, he bent out a little too far and fell into the murky water. Instantly, the cold of the water was such a shock to a small creature that had not yet grown his adult coat. He dropped under the surface of the water, gulping hard and tried to move his paws in a swimming action but he was so stunned by the cold that he panicked and started to squeak. Luckily, Dad was not too far away and rescued him from the water seconds later, but since that point, Dexter and water have become serious enemies.

On many occasions, Dood had tried to combat the problem. He had read on the interweb how to overcome fears by gentle introduction to the feared object in a safe and comfortable environment. So Dood had taken him up to the duck pond in the middle of the woods, where he knew Dexter enjoyed taking in the most wonderful sniffs, and they had tried on many occasions to learn how to swim. I know you are thinking dogs just know how to swim, like us humans know how to walk, and Dexter could be the world's best swimmer - he just couldn't get into the water without having a major panic! When confronted with the pond, he sat at the shore of the expanse of water in his favourite spot and just watched. Annoyingly, he observed other puppies launching themselves from the side of the pond at speed to chase sticks floating on the water and some of the cocky ones even spun in the air before landing (a bit like the high board in the diving events at the Olympics).

On one of the many occasions when they were alone and couldn't be heard by other walkers, Dood sat by his friend encouragingly, "Look Dexter once you are in there, you will love it, your paws will know exactly how to swim. They will just move once you are in, trust me!" he pleaded calmly, with his feet hanging over the side of the pond into the warm water below. This pond was important to Dexter and Dood, it was where they had 'found' their magic powers. The duo weren't exactly sure how; but Dexter's nose had somehow come into contact with a magical puzzle piece and the rest as they say is history!

"It's just, when I put my paw in the water, I start to shiver and feel so sick, I just can't do it Dood, it is so frightening!" Dexter replied, pacing along the water's edge looking for a 'comfortable' place to enter the water. Up and down he paced, sitting, pawing the water, squeaking with fear and constantly shaking. At one point he even woofed at the water in pure frustration.

Helpfully Dood threw some of his favourite small sticks into the water, just out of his reach to encourage him to take the 'leap of faith'. After about half an hour, Dexter was in the water up to his knees and elbows, constantly pacing and squeaking. "Dood can we go now! Look how far I've come! I'm half way there, look at how far the water is up my legs, I'm almost swimming!" he tried to convince his sceptical friend.

"Exactly, look how far you have come Dex...a little further and you will be swimming... You can't back out now you have come this far!' Dood explained confidentially, indicating to Dexter that they weren't going anywhere until he had had a little try!

Finally as the sun started to set that day, Dood got to his feet and threw himself into the water and pretended he was drowning, "Help, Dexter help... I've banged my foot on the way in - I need you to help me!' Dood screamed. Dexter ignored his friend, believing it was yet another of his Oscar award winning performances. Up and down in the water Dood moved, Dexter observed his friend, finding the whole situation quite amusing. As the seconds ticked by, Dood came to the surface less frequently and Dexter began to panic that he actually could be injured and wasn't faking after all.

Back and forth Dexter paced, shaking and woofing, until finally he took an almighty deep breath, blocked off his nose holes by breathing in, closed his eyes and jumped timidly about thirty centimetres into the water beyond. A pathetic splash later and expecting to die, Dexter lay there floating like a piece of driftwood. However his legs had a different idea. Instantaneously they took over, moving in a circular motion like he was an Olympic swimmer; he stretched his head high above the water and began to move towards his buddy. Eventually he opened one eye to find Dood standing in the water that was waist high even on dinky Dood, he was smiling and clapping so loudly the nearby birds joined in with a chorus of chirps!

"You have done it buddy, you can swim!" Dood shouted to a treading water Dexter.

"Erm, I guess but I don't like it one bit... I'm heading for dry land.." he answered in a squeaky high pitched voice. He expertly turned in the water and headed for land. Quickly, he walked ashore, stood on dry land, and completed a full body shake including straight tail and ear flapping propeller head. To finish he finally shook his back paws by stretching and shaking each in turn until he was sufficiently dry and headed for home without even a second glance at his buddy, who was swimming back to shore.

As they walked home dripping excess water and pond remnants along the windy tracks, Dood knew that Dexter was secretly quite proud of himself as he walked with a spring in his step but he would have to choose his moment to bring up this tricky subject again.

Dexter dog brave and strong. He sat there looking for ever so long!

CHAPTER 30

"Come on Dexter it's SATURDAY! My most favourite day of the week and it's time to do some extra 'superhero retrieval of entrapped people' practise. As we were so amazing, I have a superb plan that will test us, but after last night's success I am confident that we will succeed with shining colours!" Dood exclaimed using his hands to do the talking with excitement, climbing down the ladder that allowed access to the top of the bed.

Sleepily Dexter followed his master as if he were a fireman responding to a fire call by placing all four paws; two either side of the wooden outer sections of the ladder and slid expertly head first down the ramp. Routinely the usual morning ritual prepared him for the day ahead: consisting of a full body rub and head shake on his rug, ensured he was ready for whatever adventure came his way. Periodically forgotten was the shared dream moments before, however it was ingrained in their mind for many further conversations to come.

Proudly, Dood opened the wardrobe doors and pulled his costume off its peg by the shoulder; it held pride of place on the back of the door. Before he had time to put it on, Dood was interrupted.

"No chance, Dood it's daylight! I only went out dressed like that last night knowing that nobody I know would see me! And before you try to convince me otherwise, no, no and finally NO!" Dexter sat down on the rug and folded his front paws like a petulant child, placing his most adamant stubborn expression on his face.

Begrudgingly, Dood closed the door of the wardrobe, "I wasn't going to even ask my friend, I want us to be even better before we wear these costumes once more! Ha Ha! You've got me so very wrong!" Dood lied, disappointment rising within him, going bright red in the face.

Back turned away from him, Dexter prodded Dood in his ribs but Dood didn't turn round, "Yes you did," he mocked with a wry smile on his jowls, "You are obsessed with dressing up... You should be in the West End, never mind a superhero!"

Dood turned around slowly with a sorrowful expression across his face and his arms hung woefully by his side, "Sometimes Dexter I think this superhero thing should just be me and not you... You are so very ungrateful!" he plotted, trying a different technique to get what he wanted.

Flummoxed, Dexter sat and moved his head side to side looking into Dood's face, thinking. "I'm sorry buddy, I just don't like feeling embarrassed in front of the other creatures on the block! Surely you understand... How many other puppies, kitties or even tortoises do you know that wear clothes?" he quizzed, pleadingly.

Immediately, Dood retaliated, "If we go out this time without costumes and our practise run is just as successful as yesterday's... do you agree to wear your costume from that time forwards, when we are out on superhero business?'"

Thinking hard for a reason to object, Dexter unfolded his arms and lay down placing his 'thinking' head on his outstretched front paws. He knew that if he agreed then he would have to spend most of his free time dressed up in a cape. However he would never tell Dood that he actually quite liked his new costume and if they gained credibility as superheroes, completing excellent recoveries without any issues, then perhaps he was quite happy to be seen out in his new outfit. A considered back up plan could be to either cover himself in flour, pieces of bush or simply lose bits of the costume whilst flying, but he would keep these to himself just now.

Standing upright once more and ready for adventure, Dexter responded enthusiastically, "That sounds like a great deal to me! Hopefully after more practise today we will be ready to let the whole world know all about us, as we will put the other superheroes out there to shame Dood! I can't wait!"

This was like pure magic to Dood's ears! His best buddy was back to his ridiculously amazing best and they were about to complete more practice rescues that would then lead them into real life rescues and that would equate to notoriety like no one else! Dood could not be any happier!

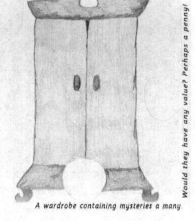

A wardrobe containing mysteries a many.

Would they have any value? Perhaps a penny!

114

CHAPTER 31

That particular Saturday morning was a frosty and icy one! A blanket of snow covered the roads and paths causing a mild panic amongst shoppers and paper-round boys and girls! Begrudgingly, Dood had placed his hat, coat and gloves over his clothes and adventure belt, due to the icy wind and Dood had strapped Dexter's loyal red coat to his buddy, to keep out the draughts. Scarily, to add additional challenge to their developing rescue skills today, was the unwelcome problem of ice and frost! Dood knew, after watching the hourly news updates on the television, that as soon as ice and snow arrived yearly, a mild panic arose across the town and country alike. Strangely (as it happens every year) England, where Dood lived, was never prepared for the cold snap unlike other countries nearby. Therefore Dood surmised that there would be some 'real' problems for them to solve, that were definitely not life threatening and, if all went to plan, a few of the local people would begin to stand by and take note of the new superheroes living in their town.

"Right the plan is as follows, we are going to fly up to the roof of the town hall," Dood explained as they walked along the paths heading for the local town that was five minutes stroll away. "From there we can peer over the ledge and observe the whole centre of the town... as people (potential rescuees) start to visit they are bound to slip, fall or do something equally rescuable!"

As they walked, Dexter had his nose stuck to the floor sniffing, marking his scent with his 'happy' tail swaying back and forth high in the air. Predictably he wasn't taking very much notice of the instructions just now! They didn't visit the town too often and Dexter welcomed the smells of bacon butties, hog roast, burgers and other meaty delights. He couldn't believe his luck when he stumbled upon a left over Butcher's best premium sausage wrapped in some mouldy bread! Instantly exerting a four paw drive emergency stop, gripping all four paws stubbornly into the ice and complete refusal to move until he had munched his prize, Dood stood by patiently as his teeth began to chatter, hands placed on his hips. Due to the coldness however,

Dexter didn't complete his rolling and woofing ritual, just a quick sniff and poke with his trusty right paw before wolfing it down in one bite!

"Could the day get off to a better start?" Dexter smiled to his buddy, licking his lips like the cat that got the cream, as they continued their quest. "I feel even more superhero-like now that I have a sausage in my tummy! That is bound to help the rescuing of people today!"

After many other sniffing pauses, they finally reached the town hall which was a tall, slender ornate building in the centre of the irregular high street buildings. Both Dood and Dexter stood outside the front entrance and looked up at its height and splendour. It really was a monumental building, a bit old and decrepit for Dood's tastes, but a suitable place for superheroes none the less! Dreamily Dood had often thought that this would be a fitting venue for the duo to receive their OBE, knighthood or George Cross when their superhero status had been recognised by the world!

"I think we would be best to go round the back, as we need to find something suitably stinky to sneeze over!" Dood suggested, guiding them around the corner towards the rear of the grand building down a slender snicket at the right hand side of the red brick building.

Cleverly Dexter had refined the ability to sneeze on command when he wanted to, but he wasn't going to tell Dood that as any extra sniff opportunities should be welcomed with open arms, he felt!

Finally, one immense 'atishoo!' later, the magic took over: blues rockets, dust pouch and propellers ready, they were both so excited about starting their next adventure. Dood straddled Dexter's back expertly and searched for the dial on his neck, just as they had practised the following evening. Eventually, he found it but strangely it was in a different place to last time. It was much lower, almost on Dexter's back but luckily it was there! Dood wondered with frustration, why this dial kept on changing position, however the excitement of the next adventure took over! Rather than the insults or the simple coloured sections with arrows, this time the dial looked complex - too complex for boys! There were letters: N, NE, S, SE, E, W, NW, NE and in the centre was a question....'Can you make me work..... I don't think so?'

Frustrated, Dood just looked at the dial and his heart sank. Why was someone trying to challenge him? It felt like he was back at school. Cautiously, he looked over his shoulder to see if Miss Snitch was nearby to give him a maths or geography lecture in directions. Rather than having a mini panic (he was a superhero - heroes didn't panic over such minor problems) he puffed out his chest and remembered that he was about to embark on a fabulous adventure and something as small as a dial was not going to stop him! (Even though he felt sick to the pit of his stomach.)

"Come on Dood let's go, press up and off we go!" Dexter shouted, in such an excitable voice, "I've never been thirstier for adventure in my life!" Paws and nose readily in position for adventure!

Dood stepped off his buddy and stood beside him, biting his bottom lip, "We have a slight problem Dexter, the dial thing on your neck has letters now, loads of them and no arrows or colours, I'm not sure which to press as I don't want us to end up catapulted into oblivion with no safety net!" he explained.

"Dood I have sufficient flying confidence today that....
Well who needs a stupid dial! I feel like an expert flying
machine who could take on the world... if the direction is
wrong I think I could just fly against it.... I am...I am
AMAZING!" he bragged, which was quite out of
character for Dexter, but the sausage must have given
him extra aviation confidence.

Stunned and rather unsure, Dood hopped onto his back
once more and using his sporadic common sense pressed
the N button that was at the top of the dial, with
caution. He held on to Dexter's tummy with both arms
and braced for impact. Head held high, Dexter began to
hover slightly off the ground and the lift towards the top
of the town hall commenced. With caution Dood raised
his head and moved his hands onto the 'handlebars' to
help steer but unfortunately as he did, the dial
demonstrated what N meant. Dizzily, the duo embarked
on a right hand spin in mid air, similarly to when Dexter
decides to chase his own tail. This continued for long
enough to enable Dood to lose his grip, fly off Dexter's
back and land on the rubbish pile next door to the Town
Hall, that was ready for collection later that day.

Fortunately the pile broke his fall and he would have quite enjoyed the experience if he hadn't been trying to get to the top of a building. Dexter however was continuing to spin in mid air! His tongue was flapping outside his mouth with the force and his eyes were beginning to become crossed in his dizzy state! "Try to fly against it Dexter, like you said," Dood shouted, after he had brushed himself down to free himself of rubbish residue!

"Iiiiittttt""""sss aaa bbbiiiitttt ttttrrrriiiicccckkkkkyyyy!!!!!" he shouted through the spinning force!

As Dexter continued to spin, he began to lower towards the floor next to Dood! Patiently, Dood stood by watching and waiting, like a pensive cat about to pounce. He observed the regularity of the spins and like an experienced superhero jumped back onto Dexter's back and held onto his tummy with one hand whilst pressing the S key, with some difficulty and resistance, on the dial with the other hand.

Strangely Dood was beginning to enjoy this spinning and guessing game and had forgotten what their aim of the day was, completely lost in the moment. Dexter, however, was about to see his prized sausage again once more if the spinning didn't stop! As soon as the dial was pressed, the spinning stopped immediately and they hovered in thin air momentarily...... before the spinning started again in the completely opposite direction.

"No, Dood I can't do any more spinning!" Dexter shrieked, as they began to move.

"I'm working on it Dexter, I just have to work out what the rest of the directions do and then we can start our work...we don't want any unnecessary surprises when we are out in public view!" Dood answered, as he was thinking the dial problem through.

Unbeknown to the duo, they were being watched. Not by any nosy humans or snobby cats but from high above the town, a creature hidden in the old oak tree that had grown for hundreds of years in the centre of the town. Something white, feathery and tired had rested on one of the branches and was enjoying the spectacle before she flew onto her next destination.

Before they had time to go into a full spin once again, Dood decided to ignore the N, S, E, W direction points, as so far these letters seemed to cause problems and he tried one of the directions with two letters in-between. With slight reservation, he pressed the NE button and again held on tightly in case it catapulted him high into the air. However, beginning to smile with relief, this button seemed to do the trick.

In mid air, the spinning stopped and they began to rise gently just above the floor parallel to the walls of the towering building. Finally, Dood steered Dexter's handlebars (ears), to the left and they hovered over the roof of the building and came down to land expertly. Eager to have a quick rest, Dood jumped off his back and sat down, gasping heavily. As soon as Dexter landed he lay on his tummy, arms and legs stretched out, panting in exhaustion. He looked as though he had been scared by a loud bang or some bubble wrap (two of Dexter's most feared noises).

"You know months back I told you to search that box thing you tap away on for a manual? Did you find one Dood? Every time we embark on flying, apart from the last time, we are just rubbish! I wish I could see this dial thing and then I'm sure I would understand it... How difficult can it be Dood, honestly!" Dexter asked, exasperated about his ability to fly once more.

"The interweb that you are referring to, doesn't have an abundance of dog flying manuals believe it or not? You don't see that many of them flying about, do you Dexter?" he retorted, sarcastically.

"Every time you change into a flying machine, the dial on your neck is different... Like a puzzle! And last night's was just a trick! It was so simple and today's is a completely opposite trick! But I'm not going to let it beat us, we just have to remember how to operate the different dials that you grow!" he explained, undefeated.

"I didn't realise I was such a clever dog who could grow such amazing things, I just wish I could control it a bit more; it may make life as a superhero a bit easier!" he suggested, getting to his feet and completing a full body shake. After he had wiped the jowl juice from his face, Dood stood up too and stretched.

"Anyway, we will consider that later. We've worked it out for now.. so until it's time to switch your powers off we should be mighty fine for this adventure!' Dood stood, bold and tall, looking cautiously over the side of the building. He still wasn't too keen on heights and so kept a reasonable distance away.

While the snow fell upon the town, the roads and paths began to get icier with the drop in temperature. People wrapped up like snowmen, walked with care, in a strange manner trying to keep their balance. Cars were driving at a snail's pace, as their wipers swept back and forth across foggy window screens. The humans below seemed to be taking extra precautions that morning as potential disaster was averted through care. The duo continued to watch and wait and started to become a little bored.

"I thought there would be loads of issues to deal with today Dexter. Maybe the world doesn't need a superhero team after all!" Dood proclaimed, seemingly in a bit of a huff (he had been waiting four and a half minutes now!).

Glad of the rest, "Patience Dood is what you need, patience!" Dexter smiled, "There is bound to be an issue today, look at all this snow!"

"I guess so..." he replied, huffing and sitting on the icy floor.

And sure enough moments later, a young girl on her bicycle, about to collect the papers for her newspaper round, slid from her bike and became stuck under the wheels of a parked car. Instantly, tears filled her eyes and a Mum with two freezing toddlers ran over to help her.

"There we are Dood, you see patience is all that we needed....are you ready for action?" Dexter asked, jumping up and down with excitement.

With new found confidence, "Yes let's go...I've never been more ready for adventure in my life! Here we go, Dexter and Dood superhero extraordinaires at your service!" as he hopped confidently onto Dexter's back checking the contents of his adventure belt, sure not to have lost any of his ingenious contraptions on the way. Unfortunately his jumper, coat and jeans got in the way, but this was not going to stop him accessing them when danger called.

Upon his back, Dood pressed the SW button which was exactly the opposite of the button that he pressed to go up and as he did so, he noticed that the message in the middle of the dial had changed to...... 'Well done Dood, maybe you are worthy of superhero status!' Dood was momentarily distracted by the rude message of praise but pressed the button and decided not to give this much thought just now!

"Off we go to adventure, Dexter!" Dood exclaimed as his buddy expertly rose from the roof of the town hall and started the decent to the floor at the side of the building, where they had climbed previously.   Cleverly, Dexter made the decision not to fly down the front of the building just in case they had yet another disaster! On this occasion they flew down the right side without error, Dood pressed the button to take them forwards and they landed beside the frightened child in moments. Stunned, the two screaming toddlers stopped their potential paddying behaviour and stared at the strange sight in front of them. Thoughtlessly Dood jumped off Dexter's back onto the ice. This was a bit of a mistake due to the ice and snow and he started to slide out of control towards the catastrophe.

Luckily he could count on his friend to help him, Dexter instantly stepped forward and stopped his sliding movements by grabbing his hood with his gnashers as he passed. Unperturbed, Dood regained his balance, took out his large extendable grabbers with padding from his belt, placed them around the middle of the stuck child and Dexter grabbed Dood's belt between his teeth and the two of them pulled backwards. Carefully the child was released from the wheels of the car and the mother placed her coat around the child's shoulders, just as the ambulance arrived. Dexter by now was enjoying the fuss that the two children were giving him and sat there proudly whilst they fluffed his ears.

"Time to go Mam!" Dood commanded in his best superhero voice, hands on hips, chest stuck out..."Glad to be of assistance!" (he had seen this on the television). Momentarily, Dexter was distracted by the feels and had to be reminded of his role in this situation, with a prod from Dood's icy foot.

"Dexter, come on...time to move onto our next rescue!" Dood suggested through clenched teeth, with a growing audience of stunned shoppers.

"I'm here Dood!" he bounded, also forgetful of the ice and snow. As he jumped towards his mini friend, he also spun out of control but righted himself just as he landed at Dood's feet. Instantly, Dood hopped onto his back, pressed the correct button for flight and off they flew, Dood waving to the public below - a bit like the Queen herself but he needed to perfect the wrist action.

In conclusion: a successful rescue! As they flew over the town, they were so pleased with themselves. The duo began to head for home with so much confidence that they could almost burst. Speechless as they flew, they relived the rescue with such pride... but were interrupted by a rumble. A RUMBLE! Not a rumble when you are hungry; a rumble from somewhere far away. A rumble so great, that the creatures and buildings below all shook in unison. It was a strange sound and certainly a response on Earth that they had never seen before! It only lasted for seconds and the people stood still, looked around, thought they had been mistaken and then continued in their frantic movements to get out of the cold.

A flying dog hovering high in the sky. The public down below would certainly question why.

CHAPTER 32

Enjoying the amusement in front of her, the snowy owl had momentarily recovered from her extended flying to warmer climes, during her rest in the tree. She needed a welcoming warm bed for a few days and she was about to return to her usual winter hotel where the accommodation was simply of Royal standards. The owner of that hotel was awaiting his visiting families and he had worried for a while that the severe weather may have thwarted their holidays.

Old Rufus looked out from his rotten windows into the grey and snowy sky. He was a patient man but he was growing concerned about the arrival of a special visitor who was bringing a gift more important than gold, frankincense or myrrh! In the distance his wait would be no longer; as he saw the graceful wings of the snowy owl as she swooped through the beginnings of a snow storm and into the aviary at the back of his house.

Old Rufus smiled for the first time in years. He knew that the owl had brought him the greatest present that she ever could, a present not just for Rufus but unbeknown to the owl - a present for the whole of mankind.

Finally she headed home for some well earned rest. Old Rufus would make sure she simply had the best.

CHAPTER 33

As Kasper lay purring that night on his plush bed of fine linen, he reminded himself of the day's achievements: Phase one was complete!

For the past week he had used his tracking device to observe the behaviour of the shark family who were drilling holes in the ground to build an immense building, to house a family of great white sharks. On his slate he had noted when they came to the site, when they left, what depths they drilled to and how long this took. Importantly he also recorded where the pillars were stored and how these were transported.   Foolishly, Oswald octopus and Edmund elephant seal had been given strict instructions to collect the information that Kasper couldn't obtain from his tracking device: how the drill operated and which other creatures lived nearby? Why Kasper employed such a dynamic duo of servants, one would never know! Off they swam with their instructions, but neither had detective qualifications on their CV nor did they even have nosey neighbour experience; so they weren't entirely sure what to do or how to do it! Equally Kasper was such a 'bossy britches' that all Oswald and Edmund did was nod their head in agreement, as he shouted commands to his inexperienced workforce, not daring to ask questions to aid their understanding.

As they swam towards the city with a slate and pencil under their fin and leg, they discussed their understanding of their mission.

"Do you know what a drill is?" Ed quizzed, dropping the writing implements as he swam - he wasn't an expert multi-tasker with only flippers and no fingers!

"A what....?" Ozzy answered, yawning so loudly, he almost engulfed a passing star fish. "No idea buddy, but we will swim down to the city and have a little look!" Both of them shrugged their shoulders in a dismissive manner about the importance of their task, and quickly became distracted by the colour, movements and lights of the city - something neither of them had experienced before. In view for all to see, the pair swam past all of the buildings, speaking to the creatures that ran the restaurants and shops, passing pleasantries about how splendid the city was with all of its vibrance.

Eventually, some hours later, their mission was jolted back to their immediate thoughts as they swam past the sweaty sharks with their noisy equipment. The pair still didn't know what they were looking for, but they could identify a shark from Ozzy's schooling - his Headmaster was a furious shark with millions of sharp pointy teeth. Thoughtlessly they paused in full view of the workers and began to watch the activity as if it were a premier of the latest box office hit. Obviously, they noted that the equipment used was heavy (due to the bulging muscles on the stocky sharks) and cumbersome (the shark workers struggled to carry it) and span round into the ground. Additionally there was also a machine that carried the long pillars, which looked like one of the swings from the playground they had just passed, but they weren't too sure what it was. Cleverly, after watching for sometime, Ozzy had an amazing idea to draw the equipment that they saw in front of them on the slate-pad. The pair luckily found a comfortable rock with a soft plush moss cushion and tried to sketch the scene unfolding in front of them, but neither had a degree in fine art so the drawings looked like something had exploded across their slate. Alert to their surroundings, the shark family were aware that they were being watched but thought nothing of it, as so many aquatic colonies visited on a daily basis. The sea city was the only one of its kind and so families saved up all of their holidays from work and spare cash to visit as often as they could - as there was something there for all the family!

When they eventually returned home to Kasper after a lovely day out, they spent the first ten minutes telling him all about the city and its wonders. Attentively Kasper listened, rage starting to boil inside him. Within seconds he realised that he should have administered a much more stringent interview process for his workers and that the two in front of him were a huge mistake and would be about as much help as a chocolate fireguard! Kasper could contain his rage no longer as his face was as red as a tomato!

"You blithering idiots, how can you possibly be so stupid? I give you a simple job to do and you come back with a travel brochure of a city that you have just visited! Did you even see the sharks and the drill? Do you know what a shark looks like? Shall I draw one for you?" he retorted with venom, full of anger and rage!

The duo, who moments before had been pleased as punch with their efforts, hearts sank. Sorrowfully, they lowered their heads in remorse.

"S..s..so sorry Sir," they stammered, "we tried our best to find out the information you needed but we haven't seen a drill before. Creatures of the ocean don't come into contact with such things." Fearful of what would happen next, the duo didn't dare say anything else.

"Why, I should place you into my pan, boil you till you are pink and then gobble you up whole!" Kasper shouted, poking one of his diamond sharp claws into Edmund's spongy tummy. They gulped hard, fearful of their fate when Ozzy shouted, "Sir, please look at this, we drew what we saw, maybe this could help."

Unable to control his anger for much longer, shaking with rage, Kasper snatched the slate from the octupus' arm and was about to throw it across his iceberg, when he happened to glance at the strange jottings. What he glanced at pleased him; but he wasn't going to let these two off the hook just yet. In a random sort of way, the duo had drawn the drill and what looked like a crane and had naively drawn how the sharks had made it work; recording the process they saw. On closer inspection it was like a basic set of instructions but they were clear and more importantly simple to follow.

With wide eyes, the frightened pair waited for approval from their Master. It didn't come; instead he insulted the obedient creatures standing before him, "How long did it take to drill a hole in the floor boys?"

"We don't know about time Sir..... but I can tell you that the drill started moving when Harry haddock started his postal round and this was when the sun just started to peep over the line where the light blue meets the dark blue on top of the ocean. The sharks stood by the drill for a really long time, watching some kind of dial moving round, as the hole got deeper and they finally pulled it out of the hole when the jelly fish police came past at the end of their shift, and the sun had bounced through the sky and had almost disappeared," Ozzy explained.

"These two really are stupid!" Kasper thought, but they had given Kasper exactly the information that he required with a clear explanation; but he didn't have the ability to say, "Well done." So he continued with his usual strategy of intimidation and fear.

"Right well, that will do I suppose. I will try to finalise the master plan from the information that you have given me," he retorted rudely, turning his back on the pair and sitting on the floor next to his slate plan, "you are free to go now but come back here in the morning before sunrise....tomorrow is the day of action!" he continued licking his lips.

Deflated the two swam off into the deep, black water heading for home. They were unsure why their master was so displeased with them but they would try return and try even harder tomorrow to please him.

CHAPTER 34

Six mice hours on Kasper's watch before the sun rose, he was awake and completing three rounds of twenty press ups on his make-shift wooden floor. For a feline who always avoided exercise and was the size of a small whale, this was unusual behaviour for Kasper but he could hardly contain the excitement from within. As usual, his sleep had been disturbed by repeated visions of world dominance. He was no longer high above the world on a fluffy cloud; instead he was deep under the ocean, hidden from view, meddling with the heat source that kept Earth stable and warm - the furnace that nurtures and sustains life.

Propped against the wall next to his irregular deluxe four poster bed, Kasper had placed his slate plan with pride as if it were pure gold. With exact timings and measurements according to the clock of Kasper, the plan had been written and would be followed to the exact whisker. For the following thirty minutes he collected the provisions that he would need for his beastly plan to start. A metal ring, with a vast collection of differing keys, a strange arched monstrosity that had two circular pads on the end (Kasper placed this on his ears and looked quite ridiculous) and a pink fluffy cushion completed his necessary items for the journey, which he shoved thoughtlessly into a mouse shaped bag the colour of his fur.

Fit to almost burst, Kasper struggled to contain his happiness and consequently started to complete one of his strange chicken dances that unfortunately involved forward rolls, cartwheels and the odd pike jump! The whole iceberg began to shake to the thud and twist of his ample size and Oswald and Edmund popped through the mirrored surface of the water to witness a most marvellous spectacle!

Before their appearance for duty that day, the workers had panicked and worried through the night about what fate awaited them this morning. But here they were before their master who appeared, at last, to have a humorous, animated side to his personality! Prematurely, they concluded that they had obtained the best jobs in the whole world and that Kasper's nasty streak was just a momentary lapse, after all how many chiefs were able gymnasts such as Kasper?

However, their bubble was quickly burst, as Kasper completed his last full spin landing heavily on his cushion-like stomach facing his workforce as he came to a standstill. He stared at them long enough to sufficiently wipe the smile from his face and resume his usual spiteful demeanour.

"You're late!" he thoughtlessly snapped at his eager workforce, sinking their hopeful hearts into their fins. "We have so much to do today and the whole process must be timed to precision or we could be shark bait!" he exclaimed, as he regained his standing position and shook his body, licking his ears ready for action.

"Sir, we came as soon as we saw the starfishes tuck themselves into their oyster beds and switch off their lights just as you told us to yesterday," they humbly tried to appease the cat in front of them, but realised it was hopeless.

"Well I've been waiting for you, so you must be late....Now let's get started!" he commanded dismissively. "Firstly, you are going to hold one of these keys each to start the drill, just in case the sharks have been extra safety conscious and removed them from the ignition.

We are going to swim down to the building site, go to the yard where the pillars are stored, roll the pillars we need for the number of holes already drilled across to the drill site and begin our venture. We are going to drill as far down into the crust as we can, making sure we pierce it and drill into the magma (he had cleverly learnt the terminology from his text book but this knowledge was lost on his workers). Luckily the stupid sharks have completed most of our work, drilling holes just deep enough for their building footings, we just need to make them a teeny bit deeper, add the ice pillars and the cooling, freezing process will begin!"

Diligently, Ozzy and Ed nodded at the right parts of the explanation as if their heads were a 'wind up' set of chattering false teeth, clueless to what was required or how. Trying to appear keen, they caught the heavy keys with their fins and legs as they flew through the air, but couldn't help worrying about what they were being asked to do.

Without any further conversation, Kasper smiled the most dastardly smile (last seen when he was about to collide planet Earth with the fire ball sun), collected his bag of necessities and dived expertly into the depths of the sea beyond. In unison the duo glared at each other in anticipation and obediently followed Kasper into the unknown.

Like a cork from a bottle, Kasper's refined swimming technique took them swiftly to their exact location. Energetically Ozzy and Ed swam as fast as their fins and legs would carry them, but struggled to keep up. Months of survival and solitude had created an evil, nasty monster in Kasper but he was also now a very able swimmer who could slice through the water at speed similar to most of the aquatic habitants. Innately, Kasper knew exactly what he needed to do. He had spent months dreaming, planning, plotting and spying.

Firstly, he went to the place where the non-meltable ice pillars were stored. Luckily there was only a single pad lock tying the seaweed in place to secure the doorway and he quickly gained entry using one of the many keys he had collected on his key ring. Once open he directed the octopus and seal to help him roll the first three pillars across the sea bed, towards the building site containing large holes drilled by the shark family days previously.

Unfortunately Kasper hadn't anticipated the weight of the pillars. As rage rose inside him, he pushed with all his might. Ozzy and Ed pushed too but they simply weren't strong enough. Even the clueless workers could see exactly why there was a large swing device used to lift these pillars as they were so heavy.

With a roar as loud as the most immense lion, Kasper heaved one more time but he realised that his efforts were useless. Ozzy was convinced that his tentacles had doubled in length as he had wrapped them tightly as he pulled; equally Ed's tail was developing a nasty blister as he had pulled for so long. Kasper didn't have the energy to shout at his workers - he was exhausted too. Defeated he sat on the ocean floor in a grump. As always, Kasper's bottom lip had fallen to the floor in front of him and his arms were folded so tightly around his body that Ed thought he might smoother himself.

"What are we going to do now? This wasn't part of my plan. This didn't feature on my slate action plan," he mumbled towards the floor, toying with the idea of an impromptu paddy! For someone who appeared so confident, Ozzy and Ed were quite amused and confused about this sudden change of character from their leader. Cautiously Ed increased the propulsion of his fins to direct him towards the floor, beside Kasper.

"Don't look so down Sir, it's not the end of the world - just yet anyway!" he explained trying to console the kitty in front of him, patting him gently on the paw, with vast wide eyes and welcoming smile.

Kasper looked up at Ed, tears evident in the corners of his eyes, "Well galloping great one!" he retorted venomously and unnecessarily, "What exactly does that great pea-sized brain of yours suggest?"

Pain stabbed once more in Ed's kind hearted chest and he wondered what he had to do, to get a kind word from this creature. Momentarily he considered throwing in the towel and finding a job shining the oyster's shells by the churchyard, when he turned away from Kasper and whistled a loud piercing sound using his fingers in his tiny mouth.

Instantaneously at least five hundred vibrant seals manoeuvred their strong tails towards Ed, as if they had been waiting for a command from their leader. Expertly, Ed clicked his strong fins together and pointed to the ice pillar and within moments it was lifted and then slotted into position vertically over the pre-drilled holes in the floor. They lowered each into position carefully so that about one third of the ice pillar was visible above the surface of the floor. (As no one could count, they had no idea how many pillars they had placed....but it was less than a hundred!) Shocked, Kasper looked on. Moments before he had thought that Ed was a forgetful seal - but now he was in awe of his resourcefulness to complete an impossible task!

As the last pillar was dropped expertly into place, he directed the mighty seals to leave the pillars and they disappeared just as swiftly as they had arrived. "I...I... don't know what to say!" Kasper gasped in amazement.

"Perhaps a thank you and a promise not to be grumpy... Is as good a place to start as any!" cleverly Ed answered. Shocked, Kasper couldn't think of anything remotely horrendous to say and so quietly sighed..."Th...thank you!"

Quietly observing all the action from a mossy rock, Ozzy yawned and clapped his eight legs simultaneously in applause: he knew his friend was great but he didn't know he was so amazing! Pausing, Kasper took a moment to rethink his plan. Amazingly, the first part had been completed with ease, all they had to do now was drill these pillars further into the ground so that the magma layer was pierced and the cooling could begin.

"Well...we just need to start the drill now from over there so that these pillars are pushed further into the ground...." he directed cautiously, unsure that his two workers may think him a little dim from moments before. Kasper took a moment to consider how he was feeling and to give himself a serious talking to! 'Kasper you are a clever, cunning cat who almost succeeded in taking over the world... these two just had a bit of beginners luck - no need to feel inadequate, your brain (and bottom) are much larger than theirs.' He then fluffed out his fur, puffed out his chest and held his head up high, ready for action.

"Use the large golden key from your key ring Ozzy to turn on the ignition and then steer it into the first hole and off we go!" he commanded in his usual bossy tone. Confused but compliant with no idea what an ignition was the two bumbled off to the drill, following Kasper's pointing finger.

Swiftly Kasper swam over to the holes and guessed that they needed to drill down as far as they could to be sure they had pierced the molten lava. Luckily there was an obvious place to slip in the key and within seconds the drill was spinning around, lowering into the first hole.

Excited once more, Kasper swam over to the drill and rudely pushed the two creatures that were carefully controlling the steering column out of the way. Kasper had to manoeuvre his ample frame a number of times as the seat was quite small and slippy, so that he could direct the drill efficiently. As the drill twisted round, it came into contact with the exposed section of the pillar and twisted itself securely into the uppermost section, like a corkscrew into a bottle cork. Once secure the pillar itself started to twist further and deeper into the ground.

Patiently, the duo of workers sat together and watched the dim fur ball's plan coming together. After several moments had passed, Ed turned to Ozzy in conclusion, 'Why doesn't he just drill these down to just below the surface so that they can't be seen and then let the sharks complete their usual task of placing their foundation pillars on top; pushing the pillars underneath extremely deeply, letting others do the work for him! He really isn't the sharpest tool in the box!"

Ozzy yawned, followed by a nod of the head in agreement. They waited a little longer until they were so bored that they almost fell asleep; they could also see Kasper looking impatiently at his watch as he hadn't completed the first pillar to the depths that he required. At the end of his patience, Ed swam over, whispered his suggestion in Kasper's ear and after a moment of blushed embarrassment, the drill moved to the rest of the pillars to sink them to just below ground level. The drill was swiftly locked away, followed by a quick resource cupboard check, to ensure that everything was how they had found it and Ozzy and Ed were relinquished of their duties once more; able to catch up on some well deserved snoozes!

Finally Kasper also returned to his iceberg, just as the school run and shops were beginning to start their daily routines. He lay exhausted on his bed, water dripping from his ample frame but he relived what had happened in his mind and he was pleased with his progress. Once he had caught his breath, he turned on his tracking device, the sonar machine, and was delighted when he could track the sharks at work and observe the first pillar being drilled into his holes. A smile broadly stretched from ear to ear as he caught up on some sleep - in his mind he plotted phase two and he could almost feel world domination once more!

His dreams had just started to take shape when he was awoken from his sleep rudely, with his face planted firmly on the wooden floor. Something had tipped him from his bed! And there it was again...a rumble, a shake! His book was right after all. Cooling of the core was going to cause these shakes and they were called earthquakes! If the book was right and he thoroughly believed it to be... Within the next few days, months and years the Earth would begin to shrink and be covered entirely in water - 'Let's hope the stinky humans have had swimming lessons!' he thought to himself, one very proud kitty!

Scared, frightened and feeling so very sad.

Kasper was the king of making them feel bad.

CHAPTER 35

Dexter and Dood had returned home, elated. They were ready for adventure; nothing was going to get in their way. Lying on the top of Dood's bed, they caught their breath and warmed up from the cold. Breathing heavily, Dood was about to speak when he felt his tummy rumble. "When did we last eat Dex, I'm starving....did you hear my tummy make an empty noise?" he mocked pointing to his stomach.

"I did, it sounded like the water gurgling down the drain but mine made the same sound...maybe we need some sausages!" he responded hopefully. As they laughed, they heard the same rumble but this time there was a shake of the bed on which they were lying. "Ha! Ha! Very funny Dex, killer farts will make the bed shake every time!" he laughed, throwing a cushion at his head.

"I've told you Dood, I'm on fart strike....it wasn't me... It was you!" Dex replied, jumping on the cushion ready to retaliate.

Playfully, Dexter jumped with all four heavy paws onto Dood's bed, helped by the momentum he gained travelling with speed up the ladder. A full scale scramble ensued on the bed for a good five minutes, involving jowl juice, tickles and cushion fight until a rumble, so fierce, almost knocked them from the their elevated position.

Stunned and still like statues, "What was that Dexter? It felt like something I've never felt before, from a long way away..." Dood shared, still panting from their fight seconds before.

Dexter had anchored all four paws to the bedding to gain stability as the rumble made him feel slightly off balance. Down the landing of his house, he could hear the doors of his siblings rooms open and shouts of "Mum, what was that?" Memories of their last scary encounter came flooding back to Dexter and Dood and they both would be lying if they said they weren't scared, actually very scared indeed! Surely there must be some explanation... World changing events surely don't happen this frequently... Check out the history books... You'll see! Millions of years pass usually between catastrophes not months or years!

Instantaneously, Dood switched on the television to see if he could find out what was happening, as a rumble continued to be heard every thirty minutes or so. He half expected to see a round ginger fur ball on every channel if history was to repeat itself, but nothing. The television continued with all its repeats and 'Made in Chelsea, Essex and Lavatories around the UK!' that Dood knew about due to Mum being glued to, with no disturbance allowed apart from imminent death, on a weekly basis! Hour by hour the rumbles continued. Down the street, the nosey neighbours had put down their garden poking equipment and stood talking in the street, unsure of what to do? Nothing was destroyed or changed, just a rumble and shake now and again.

Dood and Dexter had wandered down into the street, to get a superhero evaluation of the problem, but they couldn't see anything strange apart from hearing the rumble, however, they were sure that it was getting louder. After several minutes Dood got somewhat bored and suggested with shrugged shoulders, "Perhaps it's just the Earth telling us it's hungry!" as he shivered and they walked back into their house, ran upstairs and cosied back under the adventure table to plan tomorrow's adventures.

He could easily drive anyone around the bend.

Dexter dog, the playful 'man's best friend'.

CHAPTER 36

Deep under the ocean, Ozzy and Ed were frightened. As they were much nearer the impact site and the core of the Earth, their world was beginning to change around them rather rapidly. As the sharks had drilled down the pillars the next morning, they had done so with such force that the pillar underneath had punctured the molten lava within. As they were made of ice, non-meltable ice too, they immediately had a phenomenal impact upon the substance that had remained fairly consistent and stable for millions of years. Fifty one of these pillars were placed deep into the core by the end of the week, unbeknown to the obedient shark workers and as each was drilled, the bubbling and boiling magma was beginning to become increasingly unstable.

As the rumbling commenced on Earth, below the surface of the water on the ocean floor, cracks were beginning to form. The magma was beginning to cool, but it was also being tampered with, therefore as it moved and circulated in an irregular way, the immense fiery liquid was looking for an outlet to spill into. It firstly forced its way through cracks that were aged and already formed but then it pushed its way towards volcanoes that perhaps had been dormant for many years. New cracks were formed in the ocean floor but also through weaker areas of land, as the liquid started to look for a new home.

Boom! Boom! The top shoots high.

Black smoke and ash into the sky.

CHAPTER 37

Old Rufus Rule felt the rumble too. He could sense exactly what was causing his teapot collection to shake precariously on their plinth within his kitchen. He also thought he knew who was responsible but would he be able to help? Creaking and aching he meandered down to the shed, where the growing members of his aviary lived, with their breakfast. They too looked scared as their friend entered to greet them. "Don't be scared my friends, I am hopeful that this is just a small earthquake that will pass...try to eat your breakfast." he suggested in a kind, warm tone.

Rufus, being the intriguing, mysterious man that he was, could sense when serious disaster was happening around him - using that sixth sense! The puzzle piece, safely returned to his cellar where it had been protected for three generations, would stay tucked away for now in case the magic was needed to save mankind once more. Even though Rufus appeared very old, when needed he could react like a man half his age... Or he could until recently! His eyes were failing him, he kept dropping things and he was becoming ever so forgetful... But he just thought it was due to tiredness whilst worrying about the owl's safe return with the puzzle piece.

After feeding his greedy birds, he hobbled back through the ramshackle back door into his aged kitchen. It looked like something from a museum of time long ago. Coal fire warmed his oven, a mangle for his washing and a sink large enough to bath a small whale in it. Around the ceiling where you might see coving in a modern house was a narrow plinth and placed on there was the ugliest teapot collection from around the four corners of the world. They finished off the kitchen in a colourful way, or so Rufus thought! While he hobbled in, he looked around the room to see most of his belongings wobbling like a jelly on a plate. As sprightly as he could, he dashed across the room towards a falling plant pot, full of his home grown herbs, and bent down quickly enough to catch it before it smashed on the hard floor. Relieved, Rufus checked that his herbs and pot were unharmed and placed it carefully back on the worktop. Distracted, he didn't see what was happening above him. The tremors of the earthquake were increasing, but Rufus couldn't hear them too clearly and his floor was concrete and therefore muffled the impact under his feet. One of the teapots toppled a little further to the left than the rest and started its descent towards the floor. Rufus' head was directly under its pathway and the falling dead weight hit him squarely on the crown of his head. Noisily he fell to the hard floor with an almighty crash like a sack of potatoes. A trickle of blood reddened his fluffy white hair and the colour in his cheeks began to fade.

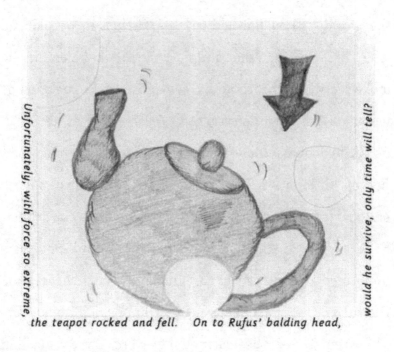

Unfortunately, with force so extreme, the teapot rocked and fell. On to Rufus' balding head, would he survive, only time will tell?

CHAPTER 38

Around the world, (I'm sure you know this stuff from your geography lessons) there are a variety of dormant and live volcanoes. Some blow their tops every once in a while, whereas others haven't done anything other than provide a rather useful snowboarding slope in the winter months for many hundreds of years. It's all to do with the lava from the Earth's core and how the parts of the world move (a bit like sliding jigsaw puzzle pieces) leaving gaps for the lava to pop through into the volcanoes. Kasper's meddling had started a catastrophe that even he didn't estimate to be so sudden and profound. While the cooling process had begun, the piercing of the core had pushed a phenomenal amount of lava out of the core all at once, in a sudden surge, so that volcanoes dormant and live had started initially smoking and then over hours had blown their tops. The rumbling that the world was experiencing was the cracking of the crust and the lava pushing its way through the surface, like a boiling pan lifting its lid and all around the world cracks in roads and hillsides were beginning to form.

Whilst some countries were used to volcanoes, preparing themselves suitably for the intoxicating ash that made breathing impossible, as well as evacuating houses as the lava rolled silently down the side of the blackened mountain, others were not prepared in the slightest. In fact some countries had never even experienced the slightest tremor of an earthquake and here they were driving along a road that had split clean in two with smoke emitting from the gap below. Not one country was unaffected! It was like the middle of the Earth had suddenly started to spill out of its safe enclosure and was now running through every possible weak gap in the mantle, as liquids do, finding a space, any space, and filling it with molten liquid of astronomical temperatures.

Mighty earthquakes make the whole world shake.

Be sure to avoid the cracks, don't make that mistake.

CHAPTER 39

Kasper jumped up from his floor and sulkily brushed himself down. Today was 'implement phase two,' the next step in his plan. However, every time he tried to look at his plan that was propped against his bed, it kept moving. Annoyingly his bed was sliding backwards and forwards across the wooden deck and his pictures were no longer straight and aligned as they were yesterday. He wasn't quite sure what was happening to his iceberg but he wished it would stop, so that he could get on with his tasks of the day.

Next, he paced the floor as best he could, avoiding flying objects, waiting for his workers to arrive but Ozzy and Ed remained absent. Evil and calculating, Kasper was plotting what he would do to his staff once he caught up with them but the thought was only momentary, as he was knocked off balance into the water by the continuing movements within his iceberg. Coughing and spluttering he came back to the surface for a deep breath before going for a swim to find his useless workforce. Kasper proved that he wasn't the sharpest kitty on the block, as it didn't once strike him that all of these movements that had never happened before would have something to do with the piercing of the core with the ice pillars! Dumb kitty you're thinking!

He wasn't gone for very long, as his eyes were like saucers when he returned to the surface moments later, breathing very rapidly. The beautiful coral was burnt and singed, shoals of fish lay lifeless in the water, seaweed was black and limp, the water was increasing in temperature and he could see burning orange liquid seeping through the ocean floor.

"Oh my goodness, what have I done?" he suddenly thought, apparently cross at how his plan had changed without his say so, "this is happening too quickly, it isn't what I planned!" as he pulled himself up onto the wooden deck in his home that now looked like it had been hit by a toddler!

Sick and poorly the marine creatures felt
The icy ocean began to melt.

CHAPTER 40

Squeaking, Dexter was hiding under Dood's bed. Whilst Dood was holding onto his bed he was trying to think. Moments earlier they had heard an almighty bang as three cars driving down his street had fallen through a crack in the road that appeared from nowhere. Worryingly, the crumblies were still out with the girls following the evening's dance classes and hadn't returned and this panicked Dood.

Out of Dood's window he could see High Cliff, the rock face that they often climbed and as he looked on, listening to the rumbles and the crashes, a huge boulder began to roll down the rock face onto the fields below with increased momentum. In the distance he could see smoke and fire from unknown buildings. His mouth was dry with fear; this was just unbelievable. At least last time, there was some warning, some clues, and some reason behind what was happening but nothing! And it was happening so quickly. Without thinking, Dood turned on his television hoping to find answers... but the screen remained black!

Eventually Dood seemed to snap out of his stunned state and muttered, "Dexter, we need to do something... I'm not sure what, but something!"

Dexter didn't move, there was a sort of sad weeping noise coming from under the bed. "Dex, I'm just as scared as you! But we must do something! This is like one of the latest marvel superhero films... Not real life!"

Sadly, the squeak had turned to a weep now but still no speaking. Quickly Dood fell to his knees next to where Dexter was hiding and laid nose to nose with him. "It's just too soon Dood," he explained, shaking with fear under the bed. "I can't go out there and try and fix this, I'm too scared... I can hear destruction again!"

"Me too! It's just my folks aren't home and the situation outside looks about twenty times worse than last time... Maybe this time we have found a real bad guy rather than just a furry orange ball, someone who may have done this kind of stuff before... Maybe a professional mean guy!"

With noises so loud, sharp and close by.

Dexter, the stubborn mule, refuses to help or try.

CHAPTER 41

Edmund and Oswald hadn't been harmed just yet. Fortunately when they saw the crack of the ocean floor increasing like a branched line through a piece of toffee after being struck by a hammer and had hidden themselves. Even though the shipwrecks were the usual playground for the sea creatures, today they would act as armour to protect the two friends from harm. Many other aquatic families had shared the same thought, cramming large numbers of creatures into every nook and cranny of the metal fortress. Frightened, Barney had led his school across the sea bed to the largest and strongest ship wreck and they hid under plates of steel hoping this, whatever it was, would pass quickly.

Hiding in one of the box like cabins, with the door firmly shut, watching the events through a circular porthole, Ozzy glumly suggested, "I know I aren't the sharpest tool in the box Ed, but all of this started to happen when we helped with that drilling. You don't think the two are connected in any way...do you?" he asked, hoping his friend would tell him he was being ridiculous!

Panicked, Ozzy had all eight legs wrapped around a metal bed frame trying to keep himself still and maintain some composure, "I had hoped that you weren't having the same thoughts as me... It does seem strange that this should happen at the same time as those pillars were hammered in. I just wish we had a bigger brain to know how and maybe then we could do something about it!" he surmised.

In silence, the two stood and shivered with fear, speechless. After a minute of watching orange gloopy liquid oozing through the cracks in front of them, Ozzy suddenly shouted, pleased with himself, "I know... why don't we go and find Kasper and ask him if he knows anything about what is happening? He could maybe even help stop it!" offering with minimal hope but really knowing that this was not going to be the case!

"That's a really good idea. We don't have to swim far but our route is where all that orange stuff is.... The coral is also cracking and shooting off through the water like bullets... Do you think we will be quite safe without armour or anything?" Ed answered, gulping inside with fear.

Panicked to the bone, the duo looked at each other, wishing that they had not woken up this horrible morning. Together they moved towards the doorway that would lead them back out into the firing line. Patiently they stood and watched, waiting for an appropriate time to start their treacherous journey. They appeared to be watching a game of tennis at Wimbledon moving their heads back and forth in unison, but the flying solid objects, fire balls and smoke just persisted.

Finally a brave Ed shouted, "Right, there is never going to be the right time to go, so I suggest we count down from 'ready' and just swim like we have never swum before.... Don't look back until we arrive at Kasper's iceberg!"

Together they began their
count, "Ready......Steady....."
and they closed their eyes,
took a deep breath and
off they went into the
battleground.

Through the porthole the workers look on.

The splendour of the ocean now long forgotten.

170

CHAPTER 42

As sneakily as a fox, Dood was lying down, commando style, on the bedroom floor facing his best friend with one of Dexter's premium pork sausages from the butcher around the corner (only used for the most special of occasions) peering under his bed, at a hiding Dexter. At first it looked like Dexter was going to ignore the temptation but as Dood pulled the sausage further away from his nose slowly, Dexter slithered forward out of his hiding place. In denial, the duo was trying to ignore the bleakness they could see out of the window and tried to think about what they could possibly do to help. A sheepish Dexter, moved forward and gulped his prize down whole, no sniff, no woof, just a scared gulp down in one!

"Right, I think we need to put on our costumes, just to protect ourselves from the heat and dust, and go out there and try to help!' Dood concluded in an exasperated manner. Defeated, Dexter was about to return to his hiding place and quiver, when he saw a further explosion of fire and catapulted boulders in the distance from the window.

As the boulders flew through the black sky like a rocket celebrating Guy Fawkes' day, Dexter noticed a blank spot in his vision. He blinked and thought it was a speck of dust from under the bed, where he was previously laid. Just to get rid of it once and for all, he embarked on a full body shake - nose to toe, spraying jowl juice once more over the floor.

"This is no time to start playing Dex, I really think we need to try and do something! You know we could always try and find Old Rufus, he would know exactly what to do in a situation such as this!" Dood spoke thoughtfully, with his back to his friend, totally distracted by the scene unfolding out of the window. If he had turned back, he would have seen Dexter systematically rubbing his face across the carpet, in a cute sliding motion.

"What do you think?" Dood quizzed, as he turned to his friend, "DEXTER! People are dying! What are you doing?"

Following a propeller head shake, that sprayed more jowl juice far and wide, Dexter shared, "There is something in the corner of my eye," rubbing his nose clumsily with his right paw, "and it won't go away!"

"You probably just need one of those things called a bath that you refuse to have except once a year! But this is no time for water!" Dood exclaimed, now pacing the floor.   Dexter shook his head in frustration once more; the spot stubbornly remained. The duo sat and looked at each other momentarily, thinking hard about the current situation they happened to find themselves in once more. "Dex, you remember the last time we went on a scary adventure, you had the puzzle piece in your vision the whole time, guiding you to its whereabouts? Does it look anything like that?" Dood suggested helplessly.

"I did wonder about that, but it seems so small that I don't think it's a puzzle piece. But whatever it is, it isn't going away!" he answered in a frustrated manner.

"Well the last time it was there, it grew when we got closer to the puzzle piece, do you remember?" Dood quizzed, growing more interested in what Dexter was saying and ignoring the events outside.

"Do you know what I think Dexter?" he explained, standing with increased excitement, Dexter didn't like the adventurous Dood in front of him, "I think that all of this is beginning to look a lot like our last adventure! You remember the puzzle piece, Old Rufus and the....."

"Yes I remember!" Dexter quivered once more, "I was so frightened Dood and you promised, and so did that old man actually, that this would not happen again and here we are months later, in a similar situation! Well I say... It's someone else's turn to save the world...not mine!" and he headed towards the bed once more in a huff so intense, Dood didn't say one word!

A magical puzzle piece in Dexter's vision.

Here's hoping there's no massive collision.

CHAPTER 43

Kasper had punched himself! Not a boxing knock out kind of punch but a literal punch to his thoughts for thinking that this rapid destruction was not a good, but rather a fantastic thing! He had stumbled across his wooden floor and ripped up his master plan. Stages two to five would probably not be needed now! In the most evil manner, Kasper had forced his ample body into his black wetsuit, complete with breathing apparatus and had swum down to the city where the pillars had been drilled. Avoiding the flying objects as best he could (but secretly feeling so arrogant that nothing was going to hit him) he had seen the results of his handiwork. Where the pillars had been drilled, there were countless deep cracks all stemming from the same point in the ground. Scarily, the ground seemed to be rumbling like a bear's tummy waiting for his next meal, smoke and orange dense liquid bubbled through the cracks.

Kasper had decided that rather than standing by and sulking about how quickly all of this was happening, he may as well speed it up a little further. Foolishly he just assumed that when all of this was over, he and his iceberg would be left totally unharmed and unaffected and he would then consider his next move once the world was free of stinky humans.

Strangely enough, there weren't any sharks or whales to block his path where they had stood hours before admiring their building work. Free as a bird, he was able to access the ice pillars and digging machines and continue his wicked plan. He probably should have been a little frightened at the swaying buildings, the loose signs and splintered pillars but he swam towards the supplies yard oblivious.

As he neared the store yard of building supplies, that remained securely bolted from intruders, the tall buildings that once housed the creatures of the ocean were beginning to crumble through the vibrations below. Foolishly thinking he was invincible, Kasper swam down to the bolted door and focused his attentions on opening it. He was pulling at the metal lock with all his might and didn't see what was happening behind him. The tallest structure that looked like a scaffolding site, which ran a track around the park for the creatures' entertainment in little coloured cars, had started to loosen at its joints. With each rumble and vibration, the bolts loosened further until the swaying structure could take the movements no more and began tumbling down to the ocean floor. The first Kasper knew about this catastrophe was moments later! Unaware, he came back to consciousness pinned to the floor with a huge bonfire of metal pieces all piled high and he was at the bottom unable to move one tiny whisker.

out.   Strangely with all the dangerous destruction,

"Oh dear Kasper!" Your luck seems to be running

there's no help about.

CHAPTER 44

After a telephone mast rudely fell through Dood's glass window, scaring the superheroes to their core, they both realised that they had to do something. In a trance, Dood and Dexter changed into their costumes, as these were the nearest pieces of clothing to protect their quivering bodies. In autopilot mode, Dood placed his gadget belt around his waist and they were both ready for action. Or were they? Dexter and Dood gulped hard as they peered through the shattered window, the rumbling continued, the pavement cracks were growing deeper and the buildings were crumbling.

As if he had snapped out of a trance, Dood turned to Dexter and suggested with fake confidence, "Dexter, we need to get out of our house, it isn't safe if windows are being smashed...I think we should fly into the sky and see if we can see where the crumblies are or perhaps a reason behind what is happening. We also might find a policeman to ask for help," he concluded, as white as a sheet.

"I wish I could think of a reason to disagree but I'm more scared here than out there at the moment," Dexter answered, the reflection of the disaster outside the window visible in his glassy eyes. "If we fly a little further away we might find that this rumbling is only happening here and not elsewhere," he suggested with hope, however knowing deep down that whatever this was, it was serious and likely to be happening throughout the country or beyond.

Instantaneously, he sneezed a rather reluctant but explosive Dexter sneeze and the magic took hold. Stunned, Dood wondered how Dexter could sneeze so quickly on command when he had tirelessly convinced Dood that he couldn't do such a thing, but Dood figured this probably wasn't the time or the place for such conversations. Rockets fired, pouch firmly in place; the two appeared ready for adventure. But were they? Deep inside, they knew that whatever this was; it was far greater than their superhero qualifications allowed and unless they bumped into Superman or Captain America for advice in the next ten minutes - they had no idea where to even start!

The two cautious superheroes hopped out of their window and elevated themselves expertly into the dusky

sky. Even the direction dial seemed to sense the desperation of their situation, as it acted exactly as it should (no tests or game playing today!) pointing upwards in the exact intended direction. Up they flew into the sky and hovered to take in the scene below them. It was as if a disobedient toddler had taken a red felt tip pen and scribbled lines parallel and circular across the Earth. These lines cut through buildings, making the brickwork crumble and as night fell, the lines appeared to have smoke emitting from them. The faint rumbling changed its pitch and volume from time to time, but it was still there.

"Dood, this may not be the time for jokes but you don't suppose that there is a dragon or monster under the Earth that has suddenly woken up do you? He may be hungry... You watched Godzilla the other night, you know what I mean?" he shared, blinking hard, taking in the view. Strangely, the people down below were still going about their business but in a more rapid way, as if something horrible were going to happen. But as they saw the cracks in the floor and the bricks beginning to tumble, the panic started to set in.

"Dexter I think it is a totally ridiculous idea, however it is the only idea we have right now! I'm not entirely sure how that idea can help us either... Any others?" Dood was looking frantically at both sides of the obstructive Dexter, through the window for the crumblies and his smelly sisters but he couldn't see them anywhere.

"The only other suggestion I have is to perhaps.... follow the jigsaw puzzle piece that is now flashing in the corner of my eye!" he added, thoughtlessly as they started their ascent out of the window.

"Next idea Dexter... That was the last disaster, please don't begin to worry me! I know you are frightened but don't make things up....Come on Mum... Where are you?" dismissively Dood answered, searchingly.

"Hey Dood, do you really think I would be joking right now.. You can feel my heart beating more than any one! I'm panicked by this whole situation... It's there, clear as day. I told you when I was under the bed that I had something in my eye... It's just grown and is now recognisable as we have started flying!" Dexter answered, turning towards his friend as they hovered. As their eyes met, Dood could tell that he wasn't joking.

181

A glimmer of hope perhaps or a red herring? Only time would tell but they had no other viable options at the moment and immediately fired the rockets and followed the puzzle piece that enlarged and flashed in Dexter's vision - but to where and who would be waiting? That was their major worry!

Groan, grumble and smash.

The window broke with an enormous crash.

CHAPTER 45

Panting, Ed and Ozzy popped up in the water that housed the entrance to Kasper's iceberg home. From their hiding point, in unison, they had both swum like they were taking part in the final of the 50m sprint, dodging and diving away from rock bullets and fiery obstacles. They were so relieved to have found the iceberg in one piece, that they hadn't considered the telling off they might get from Kasper on arrival. As their breathing slowed and returned to normal, they looked searchingly around the iceberg. The hollow white ice cube had no hiding spaces therefore it was instantaneously evident that the ice home was empty.

Ozzy blinked, yawned, "Well he is either deep in the sea somewhere looking for us or perhaps he has gone on his holidays!" he shared with about as much thought as he could muster.

"Or perhaps he has been hurt by some of the objects below; he cannot swim half as carefully as we can and won't be able to dodge the objects. I guess we should be worried, but not enough to go back through that battle zone. We'll wait a little and hopefully he will return," he suggested like a sergeant major, enthusiastically but without much hope.

Lazily, Ozzy pulled himself up onto the wooden decking and stretched his eight curly legs in preparation for a quick snooze. Sprightly, Edmund moved across the decking towards the bed, table and the tracking device that Kasper so proudly watched each day. Curiously and careful to keep his eye on the entrance to the iceberg, he shuffled across to the mysterious black box. It was just a large rectangular box, with green lines that passed across the screen. However, presently it looked like a pinball machine with all of the activity below. With his nose, he touched some of the green spots as they moved, expecting them to perhaps pause or explode, but they just kept moving left to right without stopping.

Ed was only a seal pup really, three years old and extremely playful when encouraged. As no one was watching him (Ozzy had started to snore like a Gruffalo in the corner, metres away) he decided to play his favourite game of 'catch the moving object.' Usually, he refined his skills for this game when playing with the shoals of colourful fish whilst hiding behind the coral, but today he had his very own practice screen in front of him. Ready for action, he balanced on his muscular trunk and stretched his nose to check it was ready for action. In his mind, he counted down 'Ready....Steady... Go!' and off he went; poking his nose back and forth towards the moving green dots like a woodpecker forming a hole in the wooden trunk. Faster and faster the dots moved and at one point it looked like Ed was going to travel straight through the screen with his rapid movements. As he started to move his body slightly off balance, he fell towards the screen and his flipper collided with a red button placed to the right of the black box surround. Totally oblivious to the collision, he continued his game until the flashing of the button he had accidentally pressed, intrigued him enough to take his eye off the moving targets. Being an elephant seal, he had no reason to experience such devices and therefore he sat and watched the flashing light for sometime... Unaware of the fact that far, far away that signal had been picked up by boat receivers, large aquatic mammals and dogs who could fly, but would any of them take any notice?

"What a splendid find!" Ed thought.

Lacking popcorn - he should have bought!

CHAPTER 46

High in the sky the superheroes flew. Firstly, they rose into the duskiness above their house and hovered to take in the full expanse of the events below. It was a strange sensation. So far, the world below was relatively undamaged. Deep cracks and grooves had appeared in the ground which had stopped people going about their business quite as quickly. Annoyingly these cracks did not appear to care whether there was a church, school or supermarket built on top of it and therefore the buildings had started to crack and become unstable. A panic had commenced, but it was like everyone was waiting for something far more immense to happen.

"Right.... follow that puzzle piece Dexter and let's see if it helps us!" Dood plotted, pointing into the nothingness above, turning away from the disastrous, evolving situation behind him. Even the dusky sky appeared angry, everything around him appeared scary but he had to find his one percent bravery from within, from wherever it was hiding. "Let's go!" he chortled to a hovering Dexter.

Impatiently, Dood dug his knees into Dexter's sides (he had seen and noted this during his last Indiana Jones' film fest!) to get them moving but they remained in a hovered state. Exasperated, Dood grabbed Dexter's velvety ears and gave them a little tug, "Come on Dex, what's up? Are you asleep?" Stubbornly Dex remained frozen to his hovering spot as if in a trance. It was impossible for Dood to see Dexter's eyes from his rear position, even though he tried and almost became unbalanced, but he assumed that he had become somehow frozen to the spot!

With extreme impatience, Dood grabbed both ears with his hands and gave them a less gentle tug, to gain Dexter's attention. "Ouch! What are you doing? Call yourself a responsible owner... I've seen those adverts on the television about cruelty to animals...!" he squeaked, but snapped out of whatever trance he was in.

"Dood, I have the most awful headache...dogs don't usually get headaches but there is a pain in my ears making my head shake and it only began as I started to hover. It is really painful... objects in my vision and ringing in my ears... Is this really what being a superhero is all about? I'm not so sure!" Dexter shouted, appearing wounded and disheartened.

Eager to get moving and put some distance between themselves and the disaster below, "Dex, let's not get distracted by other things just now, we have to follow the puzzle piece and it helped us last time so I think we should stick to that right now... Try and ignore the ringing. You have probably got a fly in your flappy ears!" he jested.

Without resistance, Dexter strangely didn't respond and moved further into the night sky away from his home and planet Earth. As they rose in height, Dexter steered himself towards the left as he responded to the puzzle piece flashing in his vision. Without hope, the duo tried to ignore what they saw below them. Cracks, deep and destructive had formed across every land mass that they could see and the buildings were smoking as explosions took hold. Fortunately they could not see the people below, as they feared that already humans had to be injured at best and at worst lost their lives from what was happening below.

"This noise in my ears is getting louder as I fly Dood, do you think this has something to do with this problem too? What could it mean?" Dexter shouted to Dood, as they flew at speed.

Out of breath from the cold night sky, fear and fright, Dood answered, "I think anything is possible right now, but we don't know what it means, so try to ignore it and stay focused on our flying!" We will let you into a secret: the noise that Dexter could hear...you guessed it! It was the emergency button that had been triggered by Ed below the ocean, but Dexter did not know what it meant and unfortunately we can't climb into the adventure and tell him.

Moments later, the pair started to reduce in speed and height, as they came across a vast wood with a thick abundance of tall trees. Strangely, Dood did not press the steering button, he just held on and watched in amazement as his frightened friend just knew what to do. If the situation hadn't been quite so dire, he would have organised a party, 'well done' sticker or at least a round of applause to show how proud he was of his furry friend.

High above an enchanted wood.

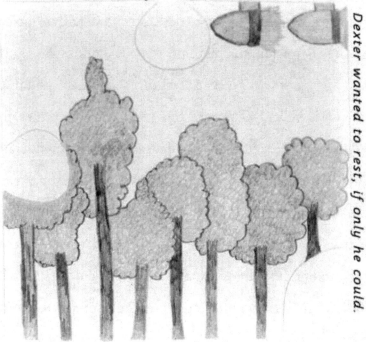

Dexter wanted to rest, if only he could.

CHAPTER 47

Kasper was scared. As he wasn't a native aquatic creature, he knew very soon that he was going to run out of air and he couldn't do one thing about it. From his stuck position, he had tried to squirm and wriggle out of the metal jail surrounding him. Additionally, he had shouted to the panicked creatures as they swam past him. However they were too frightened to pause for a moment to help him as they feared for their own lives.

Another major problem, to the right of Kasper, was a crack. A crack that was creaking and moving towards him with increasing speed and he could feel the heat of the magma bubbling at the base of the crack from where he lay metres away. Motionless, he thought as hard as he could of a way out of this situation, however nothing came to mind. Incidentally, he found it rather ironic that his plan for world domination was in fact never going to come true and his meddling was going to rid him from this planet too and that made Kasper cross! So cross!

A crack crept slowly towards the panicked cat.

Would it squash and kill him? We'll find out in ten

minutes flat.

CHAPTER 48

With intuition, Dexter recognised Old Rufus' house the minute he saw it. As they hovered over the woodland, the puzzle piece in his vision grew larger and flashed more intensely until they were hovering directly above the house and then it flashed once more in Dexter's vision and then POP! it was gone once more. "I think that is the house Dood, the puzzle piece has disappeared in my vision," Dexter explained. "We need to hurry... Look!" Dexter pointed towards a red crack line snaking through the woodland heading in their direction. Usefully, Dood tried to help by pressing the downward arrow and guided Dexter's ears; however he wasn't sure he was helping... But he felt a bit useless at the moment. As soon as he landed, the rockets and flashing nose disappeared and Dexter snapped out of his confident state. "Look through there Dood, that crack is coming straight for the house, we had better hurry!" he squeaked whilst shaking with fear. Without thinking, Dood ran up the path as best he could, tripping over bricks and wire fences, until he reached the wooden structure that once was a front door. It was hanging from its hinges and Dood tried to stretch up to see through the holes or windows, to spot Old Rufus. Unhelpfully Dexter tried to jump up to see in unison and the two looked like they were stepping on hot coals.

"I can smell him, I'm sure! That foisty old man smell is definitely seeping into my nose holes! Can you see him?" Dexter exclaimed, panting slightly from the journey still.

"No I can't see him, but I'm sure that I can see a pair of old boots poking out from the slightly ajar door at the back of the house... I think we should karate kick this door and get going Dex!" he suggested in his best superhero voice!

Stretching out his paw above his head, Dexter pointed, "Maybe we should just ring the bell? That is what most polite folk do, Dood," he mocked. Momentarily Dood glanced at the bell which had retired from action many years before and was now hanging from a wire, making a rather effective spider web home. Quickly he ran backwards to allow a running jump at the door and he used his three years of intense training at Tumble Tots to kick the door down! Once inside, the pair didn't really take in the decrepit surroundings as they charged towards the ajar door at the rear of the building. On the floor, was the owner of the feet - Old Rufus. Instantly the duo could tell that he hadn't chosen to take a mid day nap on the floor of the kitchen, as he had a trace of blood trickling from his head where the teapot had hit him.

"Mmmm now what do we do Dood?" Dexter asked, "I'm not a medic and neither are you Dood?" he looked on pacing around the disaster scene.

"No, but I do watch Casualty every now and then when Mum is out and the docs on there shake the zonked out guy to see if he is sleeping or not! I think that would be a good place to start," Dood explained, as he held tightly onto Rufus' shoulders and gave them a quick shake. Nothing! The old man stayed perfectly still as the floor rumbled below him. Helpfully the pair could hear that their patient was breathing and he just looked like he was sleeping.

Dexter stood up and thought for a moment, feeling a little sad as he liked this old man even though he was slightly strange! "Can I try?" Dexter asked, hopefully.

"Well be my guest.. Dexter, what are you going to do? Lick him awake?" he mocked desperately.

"You read my mind Dood, it works perfectly when I want to get your attention!" he replied seriously, jumping over to the lifeless human, wetting Rufus' face with a monumental lick that started from the chin moving up to his grey fluffy quiff of hair. Instantly Rufus roused from his unconscious state. Unaware of where he was and who these people were at first, shock covered his wrinkly face. As he blinked hard and propped himself onto his elbows, he rubbed his eyes with his right hand, appearing in pain.

"Rufus, do you remember us... the dynamic duo Dexter and Dood? You helped.." Dood tried to explain speaking slowly to Rufus like he was stupid and didn't understand English. As they spoke, an almighty rumble distracted them from their immediate problem forcing more of the teapots and plates above Rufus to tremble and start to tip. Quickly, the duo worked together to try to pull the old man away from the danger zone, grabbing a shoulder each with hands and teeth, they began to heave.

"Please stop.... You are hurting me further," Rufus yelped, "Think like a superhero - chosen one, use your power that will protect us!" Rufus whispered through strained teeth to a confused looking Dexter. Stunned, Dexter looked underneath his long nose to see the white furry chest where his pouch was once placed. Usually the pouch was only there when his rockets were ignited, therefore Dexter and Dood were extremely shocked to find the fur disguised pouch remained in its former position, even though the rockets had disappeared. Sprightly, Dood jumped next to Dexter and pulled out a small handful of the blue sparkly dust and sprayed it over all of them like confetti. This caused a transparent umbrella to form over all of them, giving them a few moments to gather themselves and evaluate the current situation.

Patiently, Dexter and Dood knelt and sat beside the wise old man and watched whilst he propped himself up, bones creaking and they helped him to wipe his brow of the blood, placing a make-shift bandage from a smelly tea-towel on his head to stop the bleeding. Constantly, the rumbling continued and Old Rufus did not appear alarmed when his prized plates and teapots started to fall on top of them; as the magical umbrella acted as a fabulous repellent keeping the trio quite safe.

Finally Old Rufus spoke to them in his wise and knowledgeable manner, "I am shocked that we meet once more, however I had predicted that this may happen. The puzzle piece is back with me safe and sound and since its return I have been able to see quite clearly what was causing the rumbling that you see all around us. Even though I know my strength is failing me, I was about to retrieve the puzzle piece from its secure home and ask for its help to solve this potential world threatening disaster."

In the corner of the room, the colour was draining from both Dexter and Dood's rosy complexion. Both of the ginger pair was feeling sick to the pit of their stomachs. Words like 'disaster' and 'threatening' were words that they never wanted to hear again after their last encounter with Old Rufus and yet here they were again months later and the same sorts of adjectives were being used once more.

"If we help you get the puzzle piece from wherever it is hidden, can you go and fix this and then I can go home and eat my meaty chunks without feeling like I'm on a bumpy roller coaster?" Dexter offered, hopeful that this problem was going to be taken from his stinky paws.

"Dexter!" an exasperated Dood shouted, "We are superheroes, have you forgotten, we should be the ones offering to help or at least support in a tiny way!" His voice was getting quieter as he thought harder about what may potentially happen to them.

"Stop, stop a moment, I don't have the energy to argue with you. I cannot solve what is happening, that is your job I'm afraid. You have both been given a special power and you should use it to help others. But I will tell you what to do and how to go about this mission and then I must get myself to a hospital. Please listen as we are running out of time." Rufus was speaking as if he was in pain and finding it difficult to get his breath.

For a few precious moments, Dexter and Dood sat beside their wise old friend and listened as he told them about the Earth and how it was structured and what had caused the magma to escape from the core.

Additionally he explained about the holes in the core from the ice pillars, the volcanoes blowing their tops, the cracks full of escaping magma on planet Earth and how unstable the Earth was just now. Dood felt like he was back at school! It was like a science lesson! One of those boring theoretical lessons that he often created the most efficient paper aeroplanes in!

After the explanation was complete, Rufus lay down on the cold, tiled floor once more and closed his eyes.

"Sir, I know you must rest, but I need to ask... How can we stop this from happening? What do we need to do?" Dood asked, as quickly as he could, fear rising in his chest.

"Whoa! We, you and me, magma, fire, water... I don't think so!" Dexter retorted, if he wasn't a ginger puppy, his whole body would have been white with fear at the moment. "I can't do it Dood, not for anyone!"

Rufus opened his eyes once more and turned to Dexter and sighed, "Dexter, you must be brave and strong and you can prevent this disaster... All you need to do is use the magic that you have been given and it will keep you safe and well, now hurry you are running out of time..."

"Wh...wh... do you mean?" Dexter answered, having moved forwards and now sitting upright and looking into Rufus' face.

"You don't need the puzzle piece.... Use the powder to protect you and the signs that you are given.... They will lead you to where you need to be!" Rufus answered before falling back into partial sleep.

"Will you be safe Rufus?" Dood asked as he and Dexter stood up, to walk to the door, aware that they were now out of the protected zone and could be hurt at any time.

"I have the puzzle piece and that will guide me and ensure I'm well.... Now go! The world depends upon you both!" Rufus pointed towards the open doorway and turned away from the pair.

Unbeknown to them, a snowy white owl had left her slumber and plush hotel at the end of the garden. Cleverly she had heard the conversation too, she watched as the pair left the doorway and followed them, maybe she could help them along the way?

Medicine, A&E and the doctor were needed.

Dood looked around helplessly "Help! Dex!" he pleaded

CHAPTER 48

Momentarily, the two stood on the irregular steps that once welcomed visitors safely to the house.

Both were speechless about what they had just heard. Questions going through their minds such as - Who had started all this magma spilling? How could they get the magma back into the core? How would they patch up the cracks? Were running through their minds until an explosion, with the depth, noise and magnitude of a fighter plane flying too low, jolted their concentration.

In front of Rufus' house, in the middle of the wood was a vast mountain hidden with trees. With a noise as loud as a siren, the top of the mountain had blown its top, rising high into the air like a cork from a bottle... Intoxicating ash filled the air and the rumbling had increased ten-fold.

Mouths open and speechless, the duo walked forward onto the rocky ground in front of them and sneezed to ignite the rockets, aware that they had to get away from the ash as quickly as possible.

As they flew, sprightly and swiftly, into the cleaner air of the atmosphere above, they noticed a white object flying towards them. Closer and closer it flew until it was almost parallel to their position. Stunned, the duo realised that it was a bird, a beautiful snowy owl who stared at them in a knowing manner.

For a few moments, as they hovered, she studied the duo, possibly taking in their strange costumes and observing her first flying dog and then voiced a loud tweet before turning and flying away into the blackness.

Speechless, Dexter and Dood paused in mid-air for a few more moments, appearing in a stunned, trance like state.

Seconds later, Dood broke the ice sharing, "Do you have any bright sparks in your fluffy brain about what we should do Dex, I'm all out of ideas?"

"Well the obvious answer is of course no! But I think we should follow Rufus' advice. I see it like this Dood, if we go back home and do nothing; we are likely to get burnt to a crisp, so we may as well get burnt to a crisp trying to do something useful!" Dood straddled Dexter's back and rested his elbows on his neck, thinking.

"I guess so... Should we follow that owl? Rufus told us to accept the help that we would be given and that is all I can see at the moment!" he mumbled in a half hopeful, solemn sort of manner, lifting his head off his hands.

"I think we should, we also need to think about this ringing in my ears! It has been getting considerably louder over the last hour, I wonder if this is a guide too Dood?" Dexter answered Dood, turning his head slightly to see his buddy on his back.

Consequently, Dood started to look for Dexter's dial, which, on finding, he realised again, it was extremely simple to follow, apart from this time the transparent cover said, 'Good Luck, you can do it!' This tiny sentiment made Dood smile and made him feel slightly more confident about what was going to happen.

Wise and old, she knew many things.

The snowy owl with her graceful wings.

CHAPTER 49

Off they flew for miles and miles, as night became day, the ash clouds and red veins cutting through the land continued; however they tried to keep focused on the moving dot in front of them. Pointlessly Dood tried to steer but the magic had taken over the flying and the journey was swift and painless. Shockingly, the temperature grew colder and the land disappeared. Miles and miles of blue, icy water could be seen in all directions. In the middle of the water stood tall icy towers that floated innocently within the vast expanse. The final resting place of the snowy owl was one of the tallest icebergs. She stood on the top of the peak and waited for her followers to appear, preening her matted feathers from the long journey.

Wearily, Dexter and Dood followed the snowy owl and saw that she had landed on one of the ice towers. Quite rightly, the ringing in his ears had also been a clever sign - as it was at its loudest as they circled above the iceberg until it finally ceased ringing as they flew directly over the iceberg. Round and round the duo circled looking for somewhere to land but there was no land within sight; just water and ice. From the air Dexter began to have a little puppy panic. The realisation that there was nothing but water, the thing he dreaded most in the world, was all around him. Loud rumbling, and slivers of ice were falling into the sea, lost forever, as the superheroes wasted time trying to find somewhere to land. Intuitively, the snowy owl moved from the peak of the iceberg on which she had perched, to another, in an apparent lesson in landing for the flying dog.

"Right Dexter, I've stayed silent for long enough now, hoping you would pluck up the courage to go near the water and land on the bumpy iceberg but you don't seem to want to go anywhere near!" Dood shouted, with a forceful sergeant major voice. "I'm going to take control of your ears and use the direction dial to land on top of the iceberg, just like the snowy owl did. Are you ready?" he whispered into Dexter's ears.

"No! No! No! I can't go near the water Dood. You know what I am like with water, I can't do it!" Dexter was beginning to shake and started to fly back in the direction in which they had come. Carefully, Dood took control of the direction disk and held Dexter's ears tightly to fight against the retrieving force to reverse. With a whimper emitting from the flying machine, Dood steered like he had never steered before towards the tip of the cone shaped iceberg. Louder, the whimpering could be heard as they came closer, "Place your tummy on the tip of the iceberg and stop your rockets as soon as you land, to allow your claws to grip the ice around the peak." Dood commanded, not giving Dexter a chance to object.

On the highest point of the iceberg, the whimpering dog did as he was told, changing his rockets back to paws instantly and he tried to grip the ice with his paws. Unfortunately a dog who is frightened, shakes like a jelly as well as whimpers and as soon as his rockets had gone, Dexter's four feet became increasingly unco-ordinated. They circled and flapped at the top of the iceberg trying to grip the ice. Sadly his weighty rear and gravity worked in unison to pull the superheroes over the side of the iceberg and they quickly started the sledging process down the side of the slippery iceberg. Down and down they slid and they would usually have loved such an experience had water not been involved and, of course, the end of the world depending on them. Thankfully Dexter's rear was first to hit the water otherwise he may have fainted from the sight in front of him.

As they hit the water with an almighty splash, the snowy owl tweeted a humorous tweet to herself... She had never seen such a spectacle before and was rather glad that only creatures with an abundance of feathers or objects with metal engines took to the skies regularly.

The biting cold hit them both like they had been shot. Both of them were hot and flustered from the journey and so the change in temperature was even greater. As Dexter's ears were immersed in water, he started to panic. As quick as a jack-in-a-box his arms and legs circled in the most dramatic fashion trying to resemble a swimming action however it looked more like he was competing in karate. Cleverly, Dood hit the water calmly, pulling out his ice pike from his adventure belt, plummeted it into the ice and then pulled himself up onto the flat icy surface and was now smiling at his best buddy! He couldn't help it! He looked so funny!

Momentarily he ended his buddy's misery by pulling his extendable sucker tool from his belt, attached the grey sucker section to Dexter's head and pulled him up onto the ice. Coughing and spluttering, Dexter gathered himself and tried to calm his breathing down before he passed out with shock!

Iceberg, lonely and standing tall.

Would Dexter land and begin to fall?

CHAPTER 50

Sleeping as soundly as a baby, Ozzy had continued his lengthy slumber and Ed had decided to join him after his energetic game with the sonar machine and their frantic swim across the ocean. The pair lay on Kasper's wooden floor snoring loudly. Startled, they were jolted from their sleep, not by the rumbling or a burning coral explosion but by someone shouting. Both Ed and Ozzy sat and listened as they heard raised, muffled voices above them. At first they were frightened as they believed Kasper was on his way back to shout at them once more and they didn't like the idea of swimming through the battleground again, not for anyone.

"Shhhh! Ozzy listen carefully, do you recognise the voice? Is it Kasper?" Ed considered and the pair of them placed their fins and legs around their ears to increase the volume of the sounds emitting through the layers of ice. Finally Ozzy yawned and muttered, "It definitely isn't Kasper as I just heard something woof and as far I understand, Kasper's purr not woof!" he explained ingeniously!

Stunned by his brilliance, Ed was unsure how to respond but he was quite right.... So who were the owners of the voices above?

"Ozzy, I think we should swim under the iceberg and see who our visitors are! For all we know they might be scarier than Kasper and if so, I think we need to scarper quickly!" Ed pointed out to Ozzy, hopeful that the voices might belong to kind, thoughtful people for once as they had been lacking in the ocean for a while!

As usual, Ozzy yawned and stretched his eight spindly legs before diving into the water below him. His partner followed him and they swam the few metres around the iceberg, being sure to avoid any dangerous fiery pellets and surfaced just a short distance away from the visitors.

Ozzy and Ed's first view of the latest and greatest superhero team was not as overwhelmingly positive as the superheroes would have liked. In stunned silence, the two had surfaced from the water at the exact moment Dood and Dexter hit the water.

The proceeding minutes of flapping, splashing and cries for help before the cumbersome rescue onto the ice had left Ozzy and Ed overwhelmingly speechless. In stunned silence, they looked at each other, not knowing what to say or do and were about to retreat to the iceberg when Dood spotted them.

"Hello!" he shouted, "Hello! Can you help us?" Dood pointed to the sea creatures bobbing about in the increasingly turbulent waters.

Simultaneously Ozzy and Ed looked behind themselves, wondering if this person was talking to someone else.

"Us?" Ed answered, confused.

"Yes, we need some help to sort out this problem you see all around you.... the advice I have been given is to ask for help when it is given to me, therefore you two must be it!"

Ed was even more confused and Ozzy had given up trying to understand and started to knit his eight legs together in boredom, "Mmmm! I think there must be some confusion; we are just waiting for our master, Kasper to return to his iceberg! I'm not sure we can help you but we can try!" Ed tried to explain.

"Did you say Kasper? Is he a cat? An orange furry thing?" Dood asked, growing increasingly worried and shocked that the same evil name kept cropping up in his daily conversations.

Ed thought for a moment stroking his whiskers, "I've never seen a cat before, but he is orange and he is called Kasper!"

As if the mist had finally cleared, Dood could see what was happening in front of him - Kasper was indeed back and all of these rumblings were down to him, he just didn't know the extent of the problem deep below him.

"Look why don't you join us in the iceberg where we will be safe and we can talk some more there?" Ed finally suggested as he could feel objects beneath him accelerating at pace in the water and feared one may hit the duo who were treading water like sitting ducks.

Momentarily Dood looked at Dexter and wondered how he was going to get his fainted body into the iceberg. Surely the coldness of the water would wake him? "Would you be able to help move my friend, he is awfully allergic to water, something I'm hoping he may grow out of!" Dood requested animatedly.

Obligingly, Ed and Ozzy helped Dood slide Dexter off the side of the iceberg a bit like a surfboard. Dood had packed flippers and a mask in his adventurer's belt, as well as a snorkel, and so working like a well oiled machine, they each firmly held onto parts of Dexter's body and guided him slowly down the few metres into the iceberg, placing him with one big heave onto the wooden floor. Staggered, Dood couldn't ignore what he saw momentarily below the surface of the water. The smouldering coral and bubbling magma were causing untold destruction to the sea life!

Was it a plane, seagull, whale or dove?

High pitched voices from high above.

CHAPTER 51

Panting, the rescuers all sat on the wooden floor to catch their breath. Taking off his mask, Dood was about to speak, when he was interrupted by a loud squeak from the lifeless fur ball beside him. Sleepily, Ozzy who was curled up for yet another forty winks, almost jumped out of his pink skin when the same squeak was emitted, at a much higher decibel.

Like a bullet from a gun, Dexter sat upright and took in a deep breath; he was quivering from the cold and fear. "Dood, where am I? What has happened to me? And that stuff over there looks strangely like water to me!" Dexter stammered, pointing to the entry point into the iceberg.

Standing and placing a comforting arm around his buddy, "Look Dexter try not to panic. We are in the middle of an iceberg, Kasper's iceberg and I was just about to find out a little more about it before you squeaked." Dood spoke calmly but quickly, as the background bullet noises created an air of urgency within the iceberg.

"How did you get me in here?" he continued to ask almost delirious!

"Dexter, I love you, you know I do... But right now just BE QUIET!" Dood said in a very forceful way, so forceful that Dexter forgot to shiver and thought about his hurt feelings instead.

"What are your names? Can you tell me anything you know about what is going on under the ocean? On the Earth there are rumblings everywhere, buildings are falling and there are cracks in the Earth with orange boiling liquid coming through them!" he blurted out in the most incoherent manner.

Stretching, Ozzy moved towards their new friends and Ed sat upright as if he was about to make a ministerial speech. "Our names are Oswald and Edmund!" Ed spoke, pointing at the octopus and then himself. "Sir, all I know is this .... Kasper was advertising at the town's snail office for two workers to help him with his mission. Ed and I had just been made redundant from the local builder's yard, so we needed the work. We came along for an interview and we were successful! We were so pleased!" Ed was using his flippers to explain to the audience, who were now fully engrossed in the story. As if he was injected with energy, Ozzy stretched up onto his eight legs and continued, "then he asked us to do all manner of strange things that we weren't qualified for... he asked us to go down to the city and find out about the pillars that the Shark Teeth Building Company were using to build their new compound. He wanted to know about diggers and builders and depth and stuff that we didn't have any idea about.... But we wrote it all down for him! He was always so cross with us, even when we tried out hardest..." he said looking woeful.

Ed continued the story, "Finally, I had to summon my brothers to help drill down into the crust to allow Kasper's mission to be complete and since that time all of these weird things have happened!" He took a deep breath, "Do you think that all of the fires and cracks and coral destruction is down to Kasper and what we helped him do?" he blurted out, hanging his head in shame as he asked the question.

Listening intently, the colour was beginning to drain again, once more, from the faces of the superheroes, who now that they knew what had happened, felt even worse as they had no idea how to stop it. "Thank you for explaining that. You weren't to know what a bully Kasper is. He is pure evil and he needs to be stopped. Have you seen him recently?" Dood quizzed.

"No, he has, frankly, disappeared... I was beginning to wonder if he had been hurt as the waters below us are just like a battle ground!" Ed answered once more, as he watched Ozzy saunter across the room to a piece of black slate propped up against the extravagant bed. When he returned, he gave the find to Dood to look at, "Kasper often looked at this piece of slate, I can't read, but it might be useful to you!" Ozzy yawned, stunning himself with his helpfulness.

On the slate, the plan that had been executed was fully explained to Dood and Dexter. What was used and how. All they needed to work out now was how to stop it before it was too late.

Ozzy using his eight bendy legs.

"Let us see the plan," the superheroes beg!

CHAPTER 52

Thoughtfully Dood sat quietly for a few minutes, trying to ignore the whimpering and the snoring around him. "Ed, come here and listen to an idea of mine. You said there were pillars deep in the ground that had pierced the core where all this orange liquid has come from. So I think we need to get these out of the core firstly. What do you think?" he asked his new friend, continuing to look at the slate plan in front of him.

"Perfect idea, but how? When you go below the surface of the water there is a battleground of fiery objects and burning magma to avoid. We will simply get burnt! We are also too weak.... Huge machines have pushed these pillars into the ground," Ed answered, thoughtfully.

From his quiet position behind Dood, Dexter spoke. He was quiet and frightened, but he had calmed down and had decided, possibly, that he needed to find the strength to put aside his own fears to solve the problem, in true superhero style!

"Ed... We have powers that you won't understand, we won't get hurt and we will find the strength... We just need to work out what to do....So what else?"

"Plug the holes....!" a sleepy voice from far away murmured. "Once the pillars are out, we will need to stop the magma escaping further and so we will need boulders to plug the gaps." Ozzy brilliantly explained.

"Right, this is the plan," Dood explained with finality, "we will swim down, remove the pillars and plug the gaps with big boulders from the sea bottom. We could do with some help to get things moving a bit quicker... Can you muster some workers?" he asked looking at his new friends sitting before him.

"Absolutely, give us five swims around the clock tower and we will gather all the help we can find," Ed cheered, shuffling towards the entrance with Ozzy, "I just hope not too many have been injured..."

"Wait!" Dexter shouted as they were about to dive into the battleground. With increasing confidence, he bounced over to Ozzy and Ed and licked out some of the blue powder from his pouch. He instantly sneezed covering the pair in the dust. "Just swim, you will be quite safe now that you are protected."

Dumbfounded, Ozzy and Ed were again shocked by the experiences of the day but they realised that they did not have enough time to question why. They just felt an overwhelming confidence as they dived into the water below. Spiritedly the two swam into the depths of the water, Ed destined to find his seal colony and Ozzy the whale and shark family, who he knew would be hiding in the shipwrecks beyond. The two swum as if their lives depended on it and they were determined not to fail.

Whilst they were alone, Dood had to equip Dexter for the next part of the adventure. He needed his partner in crime alongside him to remove the pillars and to reverse the damage on the ocean floor. He suspected that trying to get Dexter back into the water was going to be the greatest challenge he had ever encountered.

He sat thoughtfully alongside his best friend and looked at the water in front of him, that Dexter was now staring at. The shaking and squeaking had subsided, but Dood knew that his friend was petrified. You know one of those, heart in your mouth, dry mouth, believing you're going to faint - kind of fear... You may have felt it about spiders or heights but water was Dexter's biggest fear.

Dood was about to open his mouth to start his water based campaign when Dexter interrupted him, "I know that you are going to ask me to go into the water Dood and I really want to go, I'm just frightened!" Dexter explained, tears forming in his brown eyes.

"I know you are, I know your feelings about water but I also know that when you are actually in water, you are the very best swimmer!" Dood answered, trying to be as kind as he could be.

As they spoke, they were rudely interrupted! The iceberg suddenly started tipping to the right, moving all of the belongings inside Kasper's house towards one side. Fortunately, a picture frame narrowly missed Dexter's head as the iceberg tipped further. The duo almost slipped straight into the water without any preparation.

Gripping onto the wooden floor, their bodies almost immersed in the water, they continued their brief conversation.

"In my belt, I have a mask for you Dexter, however, if you look over there, in Kasper's lair there is a helmet that looks like a goldfish bowl.... that will help you to breath and keep the water out of your eyes."

225

Dexter felt exasperated with the knowledge that he was going to get wet whatever he chose to do. Logically in his thoughts he knew he could either sit and wait and eventually the iceberg would disappear or he could wish for a helicopter to come along and collect him or perhaps the best idea - he could try and save the world one last time!

Full of energy, he scrambled up the tilted wooden floor with his four paw drive, collected the helmet and pulled it over his head with a secure POP! The bulbous bowl made the world look stretched and strange and consequently he tried to shake his head to place everything back in alignment. However this proved tricky whilst holding onto the wooden boards with all four paws. He allowed himself to slip back down to the edge of the water on his tummy and held on once more, legs now submerged in the icy water.

"Right Dood, we need to do this I know! Let me cover you in dust, just in case we lose each other!" he explained with more confidence. "All we need now is our hired help and we will be fine!" Beside Dexter, Dood was checking his snorkel and mask and putting some strange rubbery things on his feet (apparently to help him swim!)

In unison, through the hole in the iceberg, fifty heads squeezed through the gap; the greatest creatures of the ocean were ready and armed for combat. Also through the entrance squeezed a tiny Ozzy and Ed, "I have briefed my friends and they are frightened but honoured to help in any way that they can...tell us all what you would like us to do." Ed requested, confident he had achieved his mission.

Carefully Dood climbed up onto Dexter's shoulders to enable the audience to hear him. "Thank you for coming along and helping us today, this is going to be the mission of your life! You need to put aside your fears and help us save your beautiful ocean as well as the land above. I am going to ask Dexter, my dog.." he explained pointing to his frightened friend below him, "to cover you in a special dust and you will be protected from harm and give the strength you will need to complete the task. We do not have the time to explain, however we were given magical powers some time ago, that we need to use to complete this mission. Please be brave and work together as a team!' Dood concluded, enjoying his sergeant major speech.

Taking a huge deep breath, Dexter sneezed an almighty sneeze and his rockets and flashing nose appeared through the glass bowl once again. Usefully the furry pouch on his white chest was large and open. Dexter again licked some of the dust onto his tongue and then blew it out into the air, covering the creatures below him. They all watched in wonder, not sure exactly what was happening to them.

"Right, mission 'Pull out the Pillars' needs to begin. I wonder if you and your mighty seal colony can travel across the ocean floor and collect boulders to place in the gaps as soon as they are pulled out?" Dood asked Ed and his family who were nearest the exit.

"Certainly Sir!" the seals diligently agreed and dipped below the surface, tails clapping the water with power as they ducked below. Similarly the sharks and whales immersed themselves, too heavy and cumbersome to flip in the same manner.

Only Dood and Dexter remained, "Time to go and fix this problem Dex, you know you can do it!" Dood shared, lowering himself in the water, he looked at Dexter once more and he was gone. With fear rising inside him, Dexter took a deep breath, put aside his feelings and ducked his body below the surface of the water.

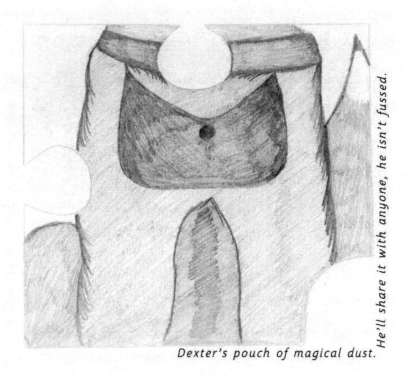

Dexter's pouch of magical dust.

He'll share it with anyone, he isn't fussed.

CHAPTER 53

What greeted the heroes, took their breath away! Shockingly, the water was cloudy and murky and had very little visibility. As they started their descent following the sharks and whales, bullet shaped fiery coral whizzed past them. Shoals of frightened fish swam back and forth not knowing which way to go. Huge cracks, significantly bigger than those on the land, were open and angry with orange liquid bubbling through them. One Saturday morning some months back, Dood had watched 'Finding Nemo' but this was nothing like the beautiful scenes he observed on the TV screen.

Strangely, Dexter moved quickly and efficiently through the dangerous water. He felt warm and confident as his rocket propellers moved him swiftly, forgetting about his fear moments before, speeding past creatures with expertise. Following him was Dood, panting hard to keep up, as he was not a confident user of underwater breathing devices and flippers. Swimming parallel to them was their work force (they looked like a rescue convoy - brave and strong) ready to overcome evil and restore calm once more! Many of the seals had disappeared into the blackness to complete their boulder retrieving mission.

Eventually, deep in the heart of the ocean, they came across the vast ocean city, after following the bubbles created from the immense creatures that swam ahead. Even in its battered and derelict manner, Dood and Dexter could see that it was a fantastic place to live and had all of the splendour of a city on planet Earth, including slides from bedrooms into swimming pools - which Dood placed in his memory to construct within his own house at a later date. Swiftly, they swam past the town hall and church yard and finally paused next to the building site of a grand, tall building on the outskirts of the city.

Instantly, they could see that this was the hub of all of the destruction. Loud, fiery, smoky orange liquid oozed and smouldered from holes in the irregular floor. Everything within the immediate area and beyond had turned to black smoulder and without the fortunate abundance of water to extinguish the heat; there would have been an instant blazing fire. As they reached their destination, the roaring and rumbling was vicious and constant, like a vintage car engine ready to accelerate at speed. Pausing momentarily at a safe distance to take in the destruction, Dexter's rockets ceased allowing him to stop and his tiny friend came to pause moments later, red in the face and panting. Leaning on his friend, "Dexter, I need some more of that dust to enable my flippers to move faster! I'm exhausted!" he gasped, whilst spluttering. It was difficult to understand what he was saying as he still had a snorkel in his mouth, but inside the fish bowl, Dexter's ears received the message. As they paused, the boiling liquid continued to seep and spray further and higher, seemingly becoming angrier by the second.

Taking a deep breath, Dexter realised he needed to take control of the situation, even though he was frightened. His little friend wasn't strong or confident enough in the water to swim and devise a plan, therefore he realised he needed to use his powers once more.

Waiting, the sea creatures obediently paused to be given instruction from the strangely dressed duo. Dexter was about to open his mouth, when he was rudely interrupted by Ed who had bravely investigated the orange holes with Ozzy, whilst awaiting their arrival and commanded, "I don't think we have long before this whole area is going to explode! As you look closer, the orange stuff is bubbling more rapidly and rising in temperature by the minute!" he was panting and twitching his head back and forth as he spoke, trying to avoid flying coral and looking for other signs of potential explosions.

Yawning and sitting on Dexter's fish bowl helmet momentarily, Ozzy explained, "If we all move towards the holes and hold onto the tops of the protruding ice pillars and pull with all our might. They appear quite loose as the rumbling on the ocean floor has disjointed them from their footings."

Barney's family and the muscular shark workers were listening intently as best they could through all the rumbling, Dood and Dexter also moved closer to hear Ozzy's quiet voice. "Ed's team has collected an abundance of sturdy boulders over there to plug the hole as soon as the pillars are removed!" Ozzy continued, pointing to a pile of black rocks developing metres away.

"Any questions? No! Let's go!" he completed, not giving anyone chance to object.

As if by magic, the immense creatures swam to every one of the ice pillars in turn and pulled them out as if they were straws in ice-cream. Their strength and the sprinkling of magical dust had given them overwhelming power and protection. Like a well oiled machine, the seals followed the workers and plugged each hole instantly to keep the magma inside the core, rather than allowing it to spill out any further. Dexter used his puppy gnashers to help the team, whilst Dood swam by, giving encouragement to the tired sea creatures and used his Indiana Jones whip to help pull a pillar out. Minutes later, every one of the holes had been plugged and the team stood and watched from a safe distance. The rumbling, continued for a short while, exactly as before and the boulders began to bubble from behind, as if they were about to be popped out of their new home.

However, an hour or so later, the noise began to subside and the boulders stayed firmly in position. The smouldering stopped and the city began to look like a building that had been saved from a severe, ferocious fire!

As if it were a feature length film, the seals, whales and sharks watched and waited as if their lives depended on it. Finally Barney moved towards the sleepy superheroes that were lying against the coral with Ozzy and Ed. "Thank you for helping us! You are all amazing and without you, our world would have been destroyed. I cannot thank you enough. We are going to start repairing some of the damage now that the core of the Earth is secure once more," he shared, before turning away from the city and swimming into the deep beyond with all of the sea creatures obediently following him.

Awoken from his temporary slumber and watching the creatures disappear into the distance, Dexter sat upright. "Team, I think we need to look around and check that no one has been hurt and needs help and then we can try to fix some of the damaged areas for these creatures. Come on!" Ozzy yawned at the same time as Dood however they followed an eager Dexter.

Slowly, they swam closely over the building site once more. Carefully they surveyed the area, looking under the rubble and burning coral for signs of life. Further away from the right of the building site, Ed summonsed his friends over to where he was searching. He had found a creature... an orange, furry creature deep below the rubble. Unfortunately he recognised him as Kasper, his former boss.

took a huge sigh of relief. The holes were filled - they were grateful beyond belief.

Barney and friends

CHAPTER 54

"No way! I knew it! I just knew it!" Dood blurted out, almost choking on his snorkel, once he realised that the creature in front of him was Kasper! The cat that had terrorised him and his dog months before! "Put the boulders on top of him and let's get out of here!" Dood continued without another thought, moving away from the area.

Woefully, Ozzy and Ed looked down at the floor, not knowing why Dood had changed instantly into an icy, nasty creature that was quite different to the person they thought they knew moments before.

"Wait Dood, we are better than that! I know how you feel, I feel the same way! But let the police deal with him... He can fester in a cell for the rest of his kitty years!" Dexter commanded, in a forceful manner, beginning to move the boulders, rocks and pillars that were on top of Kasper. Ozzy and Ed, started to help Dexter and within minutes they had removed a limp Kasper from his captive place. With a slight change of heart, Dood turned back towards Dexter and watched Kasper being rescued.

"Right, back up to the iceberg we go!" Dexter commanded and without any discussion, they all started their ascent. Kasper had been securely strapped to Dexter's back with a remaining ropey piece of seaweed and a sulky Dood followed, dragging his flippers. Whilst Ed and Ozzy tried to encourage him out of his grump, they did not know the extent of Kasper's evilness, but now wasn't the time to share this information!

Once back on icy land, the four heroes - and Kasper, lay on the floor and caught their breath. He was alive but unconscious. Creatively, Dexter had slapped him around the head with a wet slipper but he didn't respond, so he concluded that he wasn't sleeping. Sulkily, Dood turned his back on Kasper, refusing to acknowledge his existence. Sleep would be a welcome break for all of the adventurers, as they couldn't fight against their heavy eyelids due to their emotional experiences over the last few days.

Whilst they slept, Dexter awoke as he had an important job to do. With help from the snowy owl and a bag of magic dust, the world would be fixed once more. They just had to fly over the whole world in the time it took for people to rise the following day.   Would this be possible?

Dexter and Dood were entirely bruised.

Kasper's nine lives were finally used.

CHAPTER 55

Hours later, snoring loudly, Ozzy lay on the bumpy ice with his eight legs spread in the air and Ed used his friend as a cushion to aid his sleep. Dood and Dexter were cuddled on the ice, using Dexter's fur to keep them both warm. Eventually they all woke from their slumber. As usual, Dexter completed one of his full body stretches, complete with bum in the air and nose stretched. Finally he shook his head, in the perfect propeller action spraying jowl juice across the glass bowl still attached to his head, as Dood stretched his arms high above his head.

"Where's Kasper?" Dood shouted with a start, looking around the iceberg that had no hiding places. He searched the tiny space carefully and quickly but the fur ball had definitely disappeared.

"Did we dream that we saw him last night?" Dood continued shocked, "I'm sure we removed him from the ocean floor much to my disgust!"

Ozzy replied unhelpfully whilst stretching, "No he was definitely here but isn't now! Let's hope he has been taken by the seagull police!" he scoffed eager to return to the ocean, "Come on Ed, it's time for us to go and fix the ocean floor!" and the pair dived into their home once more. They wouldn't need to fix anything, the ocean had returned to its splendorous ecosystem but what a surprise would greet the brave sea creatures on their return.

The duo were left on their own again. "Where has he gone Dexter?" Dood asked persistently, "He shouldn't be left to roam the world any more. He will only come back and do something equally disastrous again!" standing and pacing the floor of the iceberg!

"I don't know! But he won't be able to get very far! The ocean creatures will learn from this experience, so wherever he is, he won't be doing very much! Let's not worry about him now!" a snoozy Dexter replied. "It's time to go home and to sleep! No more flying for me!" He stood up, took off his goldfish bowl helmet and smoothed out his costume.

"But what about fixing the world Dexter? We can't just leave those giant cracks everywhere. Can we?" he asked. Appearing panicked about Dexter's flippant attitude towards their superhero responsibilities.

"Come and see!" Dexter knowingly answered, as they walked towards the entrance.

Above them, the snowy owl had somehow increased in size, due to a sprinkling of magic dust and she would take them safely back to Mum and school (boo!). An owl taxi..... Who would have thought!

The superhero team had firmly survived.

At last the moment finally arrived.

Would they again wear their superhero masks?

Or is that the end of any rescue tasks?